RELUCTANT LOVE

Susan,
May God bless you
as you read this story!
Love, Jayne
Psalm 9:10

RELUCTANT LOVE

A NOVEL

JAYNE LAWSON

WinePressPublishing
Great Books, Defined.

WinePress Publishing is honored to present this title in partnership with the author. The views expressed or implied in this work are those of the author. WinePress provides our imprint seal representing design excellence, creative content and high quality production. To learn more about Responsible Publishing™ visit www.winepresspublishing.com.

Unless otherwise noted, all Scriptures are taken from the *King James Version* of the Bible.

ISBN 13: 978-1-4141-2449-0
ISBN 10: 1-4141-2449-X
Library of Congress Catalog Card Number: 2013904554

DEDICATION

To Ryanna, Bree, and Jack with much love!
May I be to you, as Lois was to Timothy.

ACKNOWLEDGMENTS

MOST IMPORTANTLY, I thank my Lord and Savior, Jesus Christ for His unfailing love and saving grace, and for placing the following individuals in my life:

My heartfelt thanks to my husband, John, for his continued support and encouragement while writing this book, and for listening to me read the entire manuscript while he drove us across the country.

To my daughter, Samantha, who read, and reread, and reread my manuscript, offering suggestions for improvement that have made the final product a much better book than when I first began.

To my lifelong friend, Lorrie, whose wonderful imagination has helped me create characters that will live in my heart forever.

To my dear friend, Cece, whose spiritual guidance and encouragement is a blessing beyond words.

And to Maria, whose gift of languages reassured me that my Spanish wasn't all that bad!

PART ONE

CHAPTER ONE

RARELY DID DR. Maggie Garrett walk leisurely through her department, and today was no exception. An emergency room physician, she was accustomed to rapid decision-making and fast-paced action. Hurrying through the emergency room corridor with a fresh cup of coffee in her hand, she nearly ran into Dr. Scott Devereaux as he rounded the corner, walking backwards and talking to an attentive group of medical students.

A quick pirouette, while holding the steaming cup away from her body, avoided certain disaster. The gasps from the students froze Scott in his tracks, and he turned immediately.

"I am so sorry," he said, extending his hands to prevent a collision.

Maggie raised an eyebrow. "It might help if you face the direction you're walking, Doctor." She lowered her cup of coffee, glanced at the students, and then back to Scott.

His cheeks warmed as he grinned. "Really, I do apologize. You're right. I should be looking where I am going. Lucky for me you have quick reflexes, Doctor … ?"

"Garrett."

"Maggie Garrett?" His eyes locked on hers as his smile grew wide, and he extended his hand. "I've heard so much about you! I'm Scott Devereaux."

Scott's deep blue eyes mesmerized Maggie momentarily, melting away any irritation. She glanced at his hand, then shook it. "I suppose I shouldn't have charged around the corner like that either. I'm sorry."

"No problem. Maybe I'll … uh … run into you later."

Maggie could have sworn Scott winked at her. Her cinnamon brown eyes reflected her smile through her dark lashes as she shook her head slightly. Scott turned to his students and continued down the hall. Maggie heard him say, "That was Dr. Maggie Garrett, one of the best ER doctors we have here at Eastmont. If you ever get the chance to follow her, grab it." Maggie grinned as she continued toward the nurses' station, wondering who Dr. Scott Devereaux was, where he came from, and how he knew anything about her.

The clamor of the emergency room quieted after early evening, and Maggie took advantage of the lull to relax in the staff lounge with another cup of coffee. She closed her eyes and leaned her head against the back of the beige sofa, holding the Styrofoam cup in her lap. Venturing near the edge of sleep, she did not hear the door open and close. Vaguely aware of the cup in her hand moving, she slowly opened her tired eyes.

"I'm sorry. I didn't mean to wake you. I was just worried you might spill this."

The thin veil of sleep that threatened to cover Maggie's consciousness instantly vanished, and she sat up and stared, once again, into the clear blue eyes of Scott Devereaux.

Maggie looped a lock of her long auburn hair behind her ear. "Thanks, Dr. Devereaux." She smiled weakly, taking the cup from the strikingly handsome man before her. "I suppose I really should've set it down."

"Scott," he said, sitting across from her in a slightly overstuffed beige lounge chair. "Long night?"

Maggie nodded. "Slow ones always seem long."

"I'm glad I found you in here. I wanted to apologize again," said Scott. "I tend to get caught up in my teaching and forget there is real business going on around me. I seldom get down to the emergency room." He paused for a moment, and tilted his head. "I definitely need to come down here more often. Clearly, I've missed the most attractive part of this hospital."

A slight warmth rose in Maggie's cheeks, and she hoped the light was dim enough so Scott didn't notice her blush. To her relief, her pager went off. She glanced down at it, simultaneously silencing its call.

"Duty calls?"

She nodded. "Yes. Never ends." She took a final sip from the cup before tossing it into the trash. She stood and straightened her lab coat, and started toward the door.

"Maggie?"

She stopped and turned toward Scott.

"Yes?"

"What time are you off?"

Her eyes narrowed as she prepared a mental defense. Then she sighed. "If all goes well, I'm off at seven."

"Could I interest you in breakfast? I could meet you in the cafeteria." Scott stood up and waited for her answer.

Well, I have to eat breakfast anyway, so what would it hurt?

She shifted her weight from one foot to the other. "... I'll meet you there at seven."

Maggie arrived at the cafeteria at seven-forty, fully expecting to have breakfast alone. Without Scott's pager number, the only way to let him know she was running late was via the hospital loudspeaker system, and she vetoed that notion. She opened the door to the physician's dining area, and several other doctors nodded their greeting.

If he's not here, no problem. I can eat and then go home. That might be better anyway.

Quickly scanning the room, she saw Scott at the same time he noticed her. He waved, set down his paper, and motioned to the empty chair across from him.

Wow, he's still here!

Maggie strolled over to his table. Scott rose and pulled out the chair for her. Surprised, she sat down. "I'm sorry. I had a croupy little girl and her mom was very upset. I wanted to assess her oxygenation level before I left, so I had to wait for the ABG results."

Scott gazed into her sparkling eyes. "No need to apologize. I understand completely. I had some reading to catch up on, so this worked out great for me." He gestured to the papers beside him. "Student work. Hungry?"

Maggie glanced down at the stack of papers and nodded. "Starved. I don't even remember the last time I ate." They both stood and walked together to the serving area of the cafeteria.

Returning to their seats, Maggie observed Scott slightly bow his head and close his eyes for a moment, before taking a bite of his Denver omelet. *Did he just pray?* She quickly took a forkful of cottage cheese, hoping that he didn't catch her staring at him.

"So, tell me about yourself," Scott said as he took a sip of his coffee.

Tell him about myself? What am I supposed to say?

She swallowed a bite of toast. "Let's see, I am the best ER doctor here, and students should follow me whenever they get the chance ... but you already know that."

Scott glanced up at her, with an I-don't-know-what-you're-talking-about look. He chuckled softly.

"I heard you talking to your students. While I appreciate your compliment, I'm not so sure it's true."

Scott wiped his mouth with a paper napkin. "Then you aren't talking to the same people I talk to. I understand you're extremely gifted at what you do." Scott took another sip of coffee. "The nurses think very highly of you, and that is quite a compliment. I usually hear how much they dislike a doctor, not how much they admire one. I've heard that not only do you know your stuff, but you are a very compassionate physician with your patients, and ... your staff."

Maggie felt the heat rise in her cheeks. Emergency medicine had been her dream, and she had pursued it relentlessly, putting in long hours to learn her craft, hoping to be proficient and adept at every aspect of her chosen profession.

"What about you?" she asked, sipping her coffee.

Scott grinned. "I don't think you really told me anything about you." He placed his fork on the edge of his plate. "I think I should get my answer first."

Maggie smiled. "Well, I have one brother. He is an oncologist. I like the ocean. I am—"

"Seeing anyone special?" Scott's earnest face caught Maggie off guard, and so did his eyes. She shook her head slightly and shrugged her shoulders.

"No, no one special. My schedule doesn't seem to be conducive toward an active social life, unless you count shopping with my sister-in-law, who tells me that I need to get out more."

That was lame.

Scott tilted his head. "Hmmm … I agree. You should. Life is too short to spend all your time in a hospital."

"Really? And what do you do for fun?" She crossed her arms, and leaned back in her chair.

"I usually invite pretty doctors to breakfast." He winked at Maggie, his smile exposing perfectly white teeth. "And I like to sail, play the piano, and snowboard. Oh, I also like to go to Dodger games."

"You're into football?"

Scott laughed. "Baseball, Maggie. The Dodgers play baseball. You have been to a baseball game, right?" He frowned when she shook her head. "Never?"

"Never. I've never really had any time for sports."

Scott's eyes widened. "You're kidding! Maggie, you've got to come to a game. It is a great way to spend an evening! Hot dogs, popcorn, cheering—you have to let me take you to one. Besides …" he said softly, "you can never hear a pager go off there."

He pulled a pocket-sized schedule of games from his jacket. "Let's see … they play next Tuesday." He looked at Maggie. "Interested?"

Maggie could hear her sister-in-law's voice telling her how she needed a life, but she had always found an excuse for getting out of any social activity. She let out a deep sigh. "Alright. That sounds like it might be fun."

"Great!" Scott tucked the schedule back into his shirt pocket. "We can work out the details later." He checked his watch. "Wow, I'm sorry, but I need to go. I have a class." He stood and flashed a smile. "I enjoyed breakfast."

"Me, too." Maggie took another sip of her coffee. "I'll see you later."

"Count on it," Scott said as he tossed his trash into the nearby bin. Standing a half-inch above six feet tall, his ruggedly handsome face was framed by the darkest shade of chestnut hair.

Maggie's gaze followed him until he left the dining room.

What am I thinking? A baseball game? She pursed her lips and shook her head. Elbow on the table, she rested her chin in her hand, contemplating her impulsiveness before rising to head home.

CHAPTER TWO

THE SUMMER HEAT of a southern California day quickly dissipated as the sun dropped below the horizon, and the Los Angeles Dodgers took the field at the bottom of the third inning. Scott was all arms and facial expressions as he explained the art of America's favorite pastime to the attentive doctor sitting next to him. Although his accounts of each play were thorough and detailed, Maggie's comprehensive abilities had reached their limits when he explained ERAs and RBIs. Watching the game from behind the third base line, she had a clear view of the activities on the playing field, but she still found it challenging to keep track of what was really happening.

How can he possibly remember all of this?

She savored her first Dodger dog while watching the game and had to admit that she was having a wonderful evening. With her pager off and tucked away in her purse, the game provided a welcome respite from the hectic pace of the emergency room.

"Peanuts?"

Maggie turned to Scott as he held out an open bag.

"No, thank you; I don't think I have room for anything else."

Scott frowned. "You've got to be kidding. This is a ball game, Maggie. You have to eat peanuts, popcorn, Cracker Jacks …"

Maggie started to respond just as screams and cheers filled the stadium.

"Way to go!" Scott whistled and clapped. "That was a double, and we scored two runs!"

His enthusiasm was contagious, and before the night ended, Maggie joined Scott and the stadium, cheering the home team. In the bottom of the eighth inning, the crack of bat against ball caught Maggie's attention. Sailing into the left field corner, the ball landed just inside the white line. The runner on second base sprinted toward third and was waved on by the coach. He rounded the base without slowing and headed for home plate. Sliding across the base in a cloud of dust, he put the Dodgers one run ahead. The stadium erupted, and organ music coaxed the fans to repeatedly scream, "Charge!"

The last inning was uneventful, and the game ended with a hometown victory. As the stands began to empty, Scott turned to Maggie.

"So, what did you think of the game?"

"It was pretty interesting, although I must confess there's a lot I need to learn about it. But it was fun." Maggie took one last sip of her soda.

Being with Maggie and the fact that the Dodgers won made for a perfect night for Scott. He shifted in his seat. "I've enjoyed baseball ever since I was a kid. My dad and I used to come here all the time. We also spent a summer going to games all over the country."

"Really?" Maggie pictured a boy and his dad smiling and laughing together amongst a crowd of baseball fans.

"Yeah, I still can remember Wrigley Field. That's in Chicago. And Shea Stadium in New York. My dad really liked the Mets."

"And the Dodgers are your favorite team?"

Scott nodded. "Yep. I am a loyal Dodger Blue fan. No matter if it's a winning year or a losing year, they're still my team." He helped Maggie to her feet.

"You do look quite dapper in that cap." She flicked the bill of his well-worn blue baseball cap with her finger.

"Why, thank you, ma'am," grinned Scott, tapping the brim of the cap and slightly bowing. "Shall we?" He beckoned toward the aisle, and as they exited the stadium, Maggie felt the warmth of his hand in hers. For the first time in a long time, she wasn't thinking about work.

A few days later, Maggie's ER shift was an endless procession of minor injuries, aggravated respiratory illnesses, and mild allergic reactions. It wasn't until after nine P.M. that she took advantage of a lull and made her way to the staff lounge. While pouring a cup of lukewarm coffee, she heard the door open and close behind her.

"Aha, I thought I'd find you in here!"

Maggie turned around as she took her first sip of coffee, her eyes raised questioningly at the attractive young nurse that stood before her.

"You've been looking for me?"

Hands on her hips, the nurse frowned at the doctor. "Yes, I have been. I have a few questions to ask you, Dr. Garrett. What's this I hear about you going to a baseball game?"

Maggie's lips formed a slight smile as she turned away from the fireball standing in front of her and plopped down on the beige sofa. "Really, Valerie, it was only a baseball game. How did you find out about it?"

Valerie Garrett stared at her sister-in-law before responding. "Will told me. He had talked with a certain doctor who said he'd had a wonderful time taking you to your first baseball game." Valerie paused, her tone softening. "Why didn't you tell me?"

Maggie exhaled a deep breath. "I'm sorry. It's just that, well, I … I guess I was just, sort of … I don't know, I didn't want you to think more of it than it was, I guess."

Valerie crossed her arms. "You could have sent me a text message, y'know. We are in the techno age!"

Maggie leaned back into the couch and laughed. "Text? Me? You must be kidding. I'm all thumbs with that, remember?"

Valerie frowned, then smiled. "Mags, I think it's awesome! It's about time, and from what Will told me, Scott seems like a great guy." She walked over to her sister-in-law, leaned down and hugged Maggie. "I am so glad you found time to get away from this place. You deserve so much more."

Why does everyone think I need more in my life?

Maggie's eyes reflected the affection she felt toward Valerie. She had always admired her enthusiasm for life, and watching the change in her brother when they started dating endeared Maggie even more to the young nurse. Valerie had brought Will out of his shell and given him a deeper appreciation of the world around him, which had made him more compassionate and understanding toward the needs of his many patients.

"Val, really, it was just a baseball game."

Valerie straightened up. "Did you enjoy yourself?"

Maggie nodded.

"What do you think about him?"

"I think he's nice." Maggie sipped her coffee.

"Hmm … nice. Are you going out again?"

Maggie averted her eyes from the nurse, and wondered what the proper response would be to end the interrogation.

"Hmm … I see … when?"

Maggie's eyes met Valerie's. "A week from Thursday. Something about a meteor shower in the desert."

"Oh? A meteor shower? Maybe the Leonids?"

Maggie shrugged. "I don't really know. I just know we're going to drive to somewhere in the middle of nowhere to see something I've never seen before."

"Sounds romantic. Make sure you tell me all about it … the meteors, I mean."

"Of course. What else could I possibly have to tell you about?"

The door to the lounge opened, and a nurse's assistant stuck his head into the room.

"Dr. Garrett, they need you in treatment room three."

Maggie sighed. "Be right there." She turned to Valerie. "Talk to you later … could you keep this between us?" Valerie made a gesture as if zipping her lips together. Maggie smiled at her sister-in-law as she headed out into the busyness of the emergency room.

Maybe someday I'll find the same happiness that you and Will have.

Weeks turned into months, and Maggie knew what she had with Scott was more than just friendship. His openness, coupled with his steady demeanor made it easy for Maggie to find time in her hectic life for a growing relationship.

Late one afternoon Maggie was sitting in the hospital cafeteria waiting for Scott to arrive after one of his classes. When he sat down across from her, his eyes darted around the room, and he played with a paper napkin. A few moments later, he reached across the table and took her hands.

"Maggie, I'm going to Mexico for a few weeks. My brother Ryan pastors a church in Santa Molina, a little town in Mexico. I usually go down there once or twice a year to help out any way I can. The last time I helped build the dining hall for the church, but this time I have the opportunity to go and help vaccinate kids, and, hopefully, get a clinic started. Ryan has raised some of the money he needs to get things going, and he's asked me to come and train some folks to help staff the place. Of course, I won't be doing all that this visit, but—"

Apprehension rose in Maggie's heart as she thought about how far away Mexico was from Los Angeles, and wondered how she would fill those long hours without Scott's comforting presence during the upcoming holiday season.

She squeezed his hands. "How long will you be gone?"

"A couple of weeks, and well, I was wondering … well, hoping that maybe … you'd consider going with me."

Maggie's eyes grew wide.

"It wouldn't be forever … only a few weeks, three tops, and we both know you have plenty of vacation time. It would really be a great opportunity. You'd have your own room, and we could work side by side in the clinic. You'd love my brother. He knows all about you, and thinks it would be great if you could come with me. They never have enough doctors." Scott clasped her hands tightly. "Before you say no, please think about it. I promise you'll never regret it. And if you hate it, I'll drive you back to the city and put you on a plane back home. So really, it's kind of a risk-free opportunity."

Three weeks? Three weeks working at a church? What about Christmas? What about us? Maggie released Scott's hands and sat back in her chair. She knew this visit to Mexico exemplified the very qualities that she had grown to love about Scott. But three weeks apart? She had dreamed of a perfect Christmas at home with him.

Mexico could be a wonderful place to celebrate the holiday together. And I would be helping Scott …

She smiled sweetly, leaned forward and grasped his hands. "When do we leave?"

"Four and a half weeks. December seventeenth. The Saturday after the term ends. We should be back before the end of—We? Did you say 'we'?"

"Yes."

Scott's face beamed. "You really mean it?"

"Yes, I really mean it. I'll go with you. I can't think of a better place to spend Christmas or anyone else I'd rather be with."

Scott released Maggie's hands, and closed his eyes for a moment. Letting out a sigh, he quietly whispered, "I am so sorry."

Maggie tilted her head and creased her brow. "You're sorry I said yes?"

Scott smiled sheepishly as he opened his eyes and stared into hers. "No, of course not. I was apologizing to God."

She raised an eyebrow.

"I prayed about this for a long time. I asked Him for some way to make you come with me, to help out. I just couldn't imagine that you would actually say yes. So, I was apologizing to Him for my lack of faith."

Maggie didn't totally understand Scott's relationship with God, but it never got in the way of their relationship, so she shrugged his comment off. "You know if I don't tell Valerie and Will, I'll be in big trouble."

Scott sat back in his chair and grinned. "You tell Valerie, and I'll square it with Will, OK?"

Maggie nodded.

Scott leaned over the table. "I can't tell you how happy you've made me, Maggie. If we weren't at work, I'd take you in my arms and kiss you."

"Well, Dr. Devereaux, we are, so you'd best behave yourself. As for me, I guess I better submit my leave request and start studying my Spanish." She gave his hands another squeeze as she noticed her brother walk into the dining area.

"Will, over here!"

With a few strides, Will reached their table and placed his tray down next to Maggie.

"How's it going, you two?" he asked, while sitting down and removing the plastic wrap from a chicken salad sandwich.

"Nothing to complain about," stated Scott nonchalantly as he winked at Maggie.

"Dr. Garrett?"

Both Will and Maggie looked up toward the voice that called their shared name. Another oncologist approached, her brow furrowed and lips drawn. Will excused himself and walked over to the tall, dark-skinned doctor.

"You look worried," teased Maggie, as she watched Scott's eyes follow Will across the room.

"I didn't think I was until Will came in. All of a sudden, I felt like a kid asking some dad's permission to take his daughter on a date."

Maggie chuckled. "Well, he's not my dad, and I don't need his permission. Besides, I'm sure when you explain it all to him, he'll be totally in favor of it. He really likes you, and he keeps telling me I need a vacation. Besides if your God can handle me, my brother should be a piece of cake."

Scott leaned back against his chair and laughed. "I think you're absolutely right, Dr. Garrett. Shame on me, again!"

CHAPTER THREE

WEAVING THEIR WAY through the Mexican airport, Maggie's heart rate steadily increased as her meeting with Scott's younger brother neared. Scott squeezed her hand and whispered, "It'll be alright. He'll love you."

"Remember how you felt when you told Will?" Maggie slowly exhaled a deep breath.

Scott nodded. "Yes, but –" Just then, he heard his name, and a younger version of the American doctor rushed over and wrapped him in a bear hug. Scott dropped his briefcase and Maggie's hand as he embraced his little brother.

"Scotty! I'm so glad you're here!" Ryan stepped back to look at his older brother. "You look great!" Then he turned toward Maggie.

"And you must be Maggie. I've heard so much about you; I am so happy to meet you." The young pastor took her hands in his and smiled. "*¡Bienvenidos!* Welcome to Mexico!"

Maggie saw the same deep blue color in Ryan's eyes that she often lost herself in when looking at Scott. His friendly mannerism put her at ease immediately.

"It's a pleasure to meet you, too. Scott has told me so much about you."

So far so good.

Ryan grinned. "Oh, man! I hope not everything! You'll want to turn around and go home!" He ran a hand through his dark hair, then pointed toward the baggage claim area, which, in the Veracruz airport, was only a short walk from the concourse.

In a flurry of Spanish, Ryan secured their luggage and escorted them to an old, battered pickup truck. As Scott tossed their bags into the bed, Ryan opened the passenger's door for Maggie.

"Hope you don't mind squeezing in." He gestured for Maggie to step in.

Ryan ran over to the other side and hopped into the driver's seat. Scott climbed in after Maggie and put his arm around her on the back of the tattered brown upholstered seat.

"It may not look like much, but this baby purrs like a kitten," said Ryan as he turned the key in the ignition. "And it will get us to our destination without any trouble at all!" True to his statement, the truck roared to life without so much as a sputter, and they entered the Mexican countryside.

After nearly two hours of driving through the dense vegetation, the road opened up, and they entered a small rural village. As Ryan maneuvered through the streets, Maggie stared at the tiny houses and the children playing around them. Her eyes remained fixed on a young woman washing clothes in a large tub of water until Ryan rounded a corner. Continuing straight for another mile or so, then curving to the left, the road became narrower and more rugged until the trio arrived at the site that was home to Ryan's church, the parsonage, and as he explained, their future clinic.

Maggie glanced around at the landscape, dotted with massive Ceiba trees. Their large, branchless trunks rose majestically, erupting into thick, green foliage that formed a single canopy over much of the area. Ruggedly constructed buildings, and wooden tables and benches on a thatch-roofed patio reminded Maggie of a tropical island resort where tourists sipped fruit flavored drinks while listening to the sounds of the rain forest. All that was missing was the steel drum music.

After settling in, Maggie found Scott and Ryan in the church sanctuary, standing in front of the pulpit area. Maggie couldn't make out the muffled conversation, but Ryan was gesturing wildly as he spoke. They both turned when they noticed Maggie coming toward them.

"Hey, Maggie!" Scott held out his hand and Maggie grasped it. "Ryan was telling me about a recent service where three people got saved!"

Ryan beamed. "It was amazing. I had been questioning the timing of that particular message, but I was under such conviction to preach it, and, as always, God knew best. I am so glad I followed His lead. Sometimes I am in awe at how the Lord works."

Maggie glanced at Scott, then back to Ryan. "Sounds like it must have been quite a sermon."

Ryan nodded and said, "Even though I know His Word never returns void, it still thrills me when I see His Spirit at work." He leaned against the side of a pew. "Scotty tells me that you're an ER doc, right?"

"Yes. I love the work."

"What an incredible gift you two have. I can't imagine doing what you do. I am so grateful that you both came down here to help vaccinate the kids. You have no idea how this will help us. I promise you, Maggie, you will never be the same. These people … these children … they'll touch your heart. It will be a life changing trip for you, and one, I hope, that will inspire you to come again."

Ryan's sincerity mirrored the same trait Maggie admired in Scott, and any remaining fears she had about the trip vanished. "It's already starting out wonderful. I can't wait to get to work."

Maggie's eyes met Scott's. When he winked at her, it thrilled her heart.

I am so glad I came. I belong here … with you.

After the three enjoyed a light dinner of tacos and a brief walk around the grounds, Ryan gave Maggie a quick history of the church and his hopes for the planned clinic. The moon had long risen when he remarked, "I have talked way too long. I've probably bored you to tears." He glanced at his watch. "We'd better get to bed. Tomorrow's going to be a long day."

Scott shook his head and laughed, then patted his brother on the back. "Clearly, he doesn't know the long hours we doctors put in."

"You are also supposed to be here on vacation, right? If I work you to death, you'll never come back." Ryan brushed a few strands of hair off his forehead. "Service begins at ten o'clock. After that we have the fellowship meal, then back to the church for a time of singing before we take our afternoon rest. Then back at five for the evening service … speaking of which, I'd better get to work on my bilingual message for tomorrow. I'll see you in the morning. Thank you again, both of you, for coming. I really mean it." Ryan hugged them both, then strode toward the parsonage.

Scott reached for Maggie's hand as they turned toward the row of cabins. "I helped build the parsonage a few years ago, just after Ryan decided he was going to start this ministry. He managed to get most of the materials donated, so labor was all that was really needed. There's a few people here fulltime, but most work here voluntarily, so I took some time off from teaching to help out.

"The people here were so awesome, Maggie. They worked every bit as hard as I did, and they were so grateful. I learned so much about trusting God. Since then, I've made it a point to come here as often as I can, to help in any way I can."

Maggie and Scott sauntered toward the tiny row of four cabins used by visiting missionary groups who frequently made summer trips to help Ryan. The damp vegetation beneath their feet muted any sound as they walked.

As they neared Maggie's cabin, Scott asked, "Are you still glad you came?"

Maggie glanced up into his warm eyes and squeezed his hand. "Of course, I am. It's the holiday season, and I'm with you. It couldn't be more perfect. Unless, of course, it would snow." She laughed lightly. "After all, it is Christmas time."

Scott stopped in front of her cabin door and turned Maggie toward him. He held both of her hands in his and drew her closer to him.

"Yes, it is, and you being here with me is the best present I could ever receive." He lightly touched her cheek with his hand, then his eyes grew solemn. "Maggie, if you ever do want to go home, you tell me, OK? I don't want you to think you're stuck here."

Maggie's heart was moved. "I will … I promise. But it won't happen. I'm sure of that. We're both here for a purpose, remember? And an answer to prayer, I believe."

Scott gently kissed her. "I love you, Maggie Garrett."

Maggie laid her head against Scott's chest and the steady rhythm of his heart drummed in her ear as he held her tenderly.

"I love you, too, Scott."

Scott tilted Maggie's face up, and kissed her once more. "I'll see you in the morning."

She stood in her doorway, watching Scott walk to his cabin. As he opened the door, he turned to her and waved.

"Good night, my love," she whispered as she closed the door behind her.

The small lamp on her bedside table illuminated the room with a soft yellow glow. As Maggie sat on the edge of her bed to remove her shoes, the familiar tone from her cell phone broke the silence in her small cabin. Locating it within her backpack, she saw a text message from Scott. *'I love you. Sweet dreams.'* Warmth flooded Maggie's body. Although it was slow and tedious for her, she managed to type in the words *'I love you too.'* After she climbed into the small single bed, she fell asleep thinking of Scott and the completeness she felt with him in her life.

Maggie woke to the unfamiliar sounds of the rainforest, and it took a moment before she remembered where she was. Glancing at her watch, she rose to prepare for her first church service in Santa Molina. After much debate, she chose a pale blue blouse and a simple gray suit. She plaited her auburn hair and clipped it securely, forming a loop at the nape of her neck. A dainty pair of silver and pearl earrings and matching necklace complimented her outfit. Satisfied with her appearance, she left her cabin and headed toward the church.

Maggie slid in beside Scott in the second pew as people filled the small rural church. Glancing around, she suddenly felt self-conscious in her suit. Realizing that she was overdressed, she made a mental note about changing her wardrobe as soon as possible to fit in with the locals.

Ryan stood at the back greeting everyone, occasionally pointing toward Scott and Maggie. While most of the churchgoers spoke Spanish, one or two ventured up to greet them in fragmented English, to which Scott attempted to respond in their native language. Scott was able to speak a few phrases and carry on a fairly decent conversation, albeit a slow one. Embarrassed to try what little she remembered of her college Spanish, Maggie simply smiled and shook hands. She managed to utter *"Buenos dias"* a few times to which Scott gave her a thumbs-up after her first try. *I have got to take a Spanish class when we get back home.*

As the congregation began to sing the first hymn, Scott's strong baritone voice resonated as he joined in with them. Maggie listened to him sing unfamiliar words to unknown melodies, occasionally stealing glances of his face. Sometimes his eyes were closed, but the way he sang every song stirred something within her.

There's so much about you that I don't know. Even when you sing, I can sense your closeness to God. It's like He's … a personal friend.

Scott had never really asked her what she believed, and Maggie was not sure how she would have answered that question. She believed in God, but, unlike Scott's faith, which seemed to be woven through his daily life, her faith was, for the most part, reserved for Sundays. While Scott went to church regularly, Maggie's attendance was sporadic. She had accompanied him a few times to his church, but more times than not, she was working when he attended services. He always prayed before meals; the only mealtime prayer Maggie knew was a rhyme she had learned as a child. Now, however, she always waited for him to pray before she began to eat.

I believe in God; I do, but I don't understand why his faith is so different from mine.

Maggie's thoughts were interrupted as Ryan began to address the congregation. After a few sentences, he translated his Spanish welcome into English. He went on to explain that Scott and Maggie were visiting for a few weeks to help establish the clinic, and since they were attending the services, his sermons would be bilingual.

Maggie listened intently as Ryan began to talk about Mary, the mother of Jesus, and her divine call from God. She had never given much thought to the birth of Christ, and Ryan's delivery of the story captivated her attention. Even the broken presentation of the message did not deter from the underlying meaning. The young Hebrew girl had completely trusted the Lord and had surrendered her will to His.

How could she do that? God asked her to do the impossible, yet she trusted Him completely. I wonder if I would've done that.

Maggie felt herself drawn into Ryan's message.

"Jesus came into this world to save sinners. He willingly left the splendor of heaven, fully aware that the cross was His ultimate fate. Why did He do that? The answer is in John, chapter three, verse sixteen. 'For God so loved the world that He gave His only begotten Son that whosoever believeth in Him should not perish, but have everlasting life.' God loves you, and that is why He sent His only Son to the cross, to provide a way for me and you to live forever with Him."

As the service neared its end, Ryan gave an invitation to come to the altar. A young woman rose and walked to the front of the church. She knelt down, and a few others followed.

Maggie noticed that Scott had his head bowed and eyes closed, and his lips were slightly moving, but no sound came from him. Ryan began to pray, and as he finished his petition, one-by-one, those at the altar quietly moved back to their seats. The young woman wiped tears from her face.

"Thank you all for coming today to worship the Lord with us," Ryan said. "Please plan to stay and join us for our fellowship meal." He prayed once more, and then dismissed the congregation after they sang one last song.

Scott took Maggie's hand and escorted her out of the small wooden building.

"Let's sit over there." He guided her toward an outdoor area adjacent to the dining hall where the women were already setting up platters of food on the tables.

"Should I help them?" asked Maggie.

"No, they've got it handled. We're guests to them, so they expect us to sit and wait for lunch." He waited for her to sit before he sat down. "How did you like it?"

"The service? It was nice, at least the parts I could understand."

"I'm glad. I was worried."

"About what?" asked Maggie, her brow furrowing.

"That you wouldn't like his preaching, and maybe you'd want to leave."

"Oh, ye of little faith," teased Maggie, poking him in the chest.

Scott felt warmth rise in his cheeks. "I know. Good thing it only takes faith the size of a mustard seed to move mountains, although, at the rate I am going, I won't be able to move an ant hill."

"I don't think I agree with that assessment," countered Maggie.

"I think you're biased, but …" Scott looked down at his clasped hands. "I'm just having a hard time trusting God, I think, and I'm afraid that what I'm praying for may not be His will for me."

What is that supposed to mean? He might as well be speaking Spanish because I don't have the slightest idea what he's talking about. He's always so confident about everything. Now, he's not sure? About us?

"Is it … is it us?" Fear gripped her heart.

"No. No, of course not. It's really nothing, I guess. Shall we go eat?" He stood and held his hand out to her.

Why won't he tell me?

Maggie searched Scott's face for a clue of what was bothering him, but saw nothing. Taking his hand, she stood up. As they walked, Maggie noticed Ryan watching them from beyond the tables. For a brief moment, she thought she saw worry on the young pastor's face, but then he smiled. Maggie managed a small wave and a weak smile in return, but her thoughts quickly returned to Scott and whatever was troubling him.

The rest of the day was uneventful, and although most of the time had been spent sitting in church or in the courtyard, Maggie was exhausted by the time she returned to her cabin for the night. She lay in her bed, restless, for a long time. Her thoughts roamed from whatever could be bothering Scott, to Ryan's message about Mary surrendering her life to God, to the young woman who wept at the altar during the church service until she finally drifted off to sleep, lulled by the sounds of raindrops against the roof of her cabin.

The morning came too quickly for Maggie, but she managed to wash her face in a small basin of water, dress quickly in jeans and a beige blouse, and join Scott and Ryan for breakfast. A small plate of chorizo and eggs was placed in front of her as she sat down with the two men.

"Good morning, Maggie," said Ryan, smiling broadly. He gulped down a glass of orange juice.

"Sleep well?" asked Scott as he finished off his eggs. "I texted you, but since you didn't answer, I figured you needed the sleep."

Maggie nodded as she sipped a cup of coffee. Her eyes widened a bit, and she set the cup back on the table. "Wow, that's strong! I'm sorry. I didn't even hear the phone. I guess I was really tired."

"You didn't sleep well?"

"No, I slept OK ... when I finally fell asleep. I was just thinking about everything, I guess."

"I know exactly what you mean," said Scott. "The first time I came here, I was blown away. It was like trying to save a sinking ship with a teaspoon."

Ryan grimaced. "Aw, come on, Scotty, it can't be that bad!"

Scott took a final swallow from his coffee mug. "Compared to L.A. and the state of the art equipment we have there, this place is a nightmare, dear brother, but when you see the opportunities to serve the Lord here, it is a paradise! So Maggie, are you ready to face the masses today?"

"I think so. How will this all work?"

Scott reviewed the procedures that he and Ryan had worked out, and soon they were arranging chairs and tables to accommodate the expected volume of patients. The day continued without incident, and by the early evening hours Maggie felt a stiffness settle into her body that kindled a faint memory of her days working nonstop as an intern.

It was easy for her to retreat to her cabin and settle into bed after the evening meal. Not even an invitation for a short moonlit walk with Scott tempted her to stay up much past nine o'clock. She managed to type a short text to Scott, wishing him a good night of rest, and finished her nightly duties, before falling into a troubled sleep, dreaming of a young village girl who carried a heavy, but blessed burden, and a destiny that would change the world.

The first few days flew by for Maggie. She lost count of how many children she had seen in the makeshift clinic, but felt an overwhelming sense of satisfaction in what she was doing. Working side by side with Scott filled Maggie with great contentment, even when hours went by with hardly a word spoken between them. During the infrequent lulls, she caught glimpses of Scott working steadily. Sometimes he was tenderly reassuring a frightened child, other times he was listening intently to a mother as she tried to explain her concern. No matter the situation, he never seemed to be overwhelmed by the language barrier or the constant demand upon his time. Maggie marveled at this man she had grown to love so deeply over the past few months. Even as she wondered what made him the way he was, she knew the answer lay in his faith.

Weeks ago, over a leisurely dinner at their favorite steakhouse, Scott had told her about his childhood. The son of a Baptist minister, he and Ryan had grown up in the church serving alongside their parents in whatever capacity fit their young lives. He had witnessed his parents living their faith despite hardships, careful to raise their sons to respect and honor God in every aspect of their own lives no matter what circumstances befell them. Scott had asked Christ to be his Savior as a young teen, and, firmly believing that God had wanted him to be a doctor, graduated from medical school, intent on serving the Lord on the mission field in some medical capacity. However, he had told her, God seemed to have other plans for him, and, for now, he was in Los Angeles working at a teaching hospital.

Maggie didn't completely understand Scott's convictions, but she knew they were the foundation upon which his life was laid, so they were important to her. Scott never pressed her regarding her own beliefs. Now, in Mexico, she loved attending Ryan's services. She had to admit his simple messages stirred something within her that was sometimes unsettling, but she didn't feel quite comfortable talking about this to Scott, at least not yet.

It started as a small rumble deep in her subconscious, followed by an escalating undulation of her bed that jarred Maggie from her slumber. Acutely aware of the rolling movements, Maggie's heart pounded throughout her body as she felt her bed swaying.

What in the world … ? No, no, no! Not an earthquake!

Less than ten seconds later, all movement ceased; nothing was displaced or broken. Quickly dressing, Maggie charged out into the morning sun and saw Scott talking with Ryan in the courtyard. They both smiled up at her as she approached them.

"Good morning, darling," Scott said and smiled. He kissed her lightly on the lips.

"Was I dreaming or did we have an earthquake?" Her voice shook slightly.

"You weren't dreaming," responded Ryan. "They're a bit more common here than in California, but that's to be expected, since we're relatively near a volcano."

Maggie's eyebrows arched as she gasped, "A volcano? You've got to be kidding!"

"Not kidding. But you don't need to worry. Its last major eruption was about sixty-five years ago. It's not due for another hundred years or so."

Maggie crossed her arms and scowled. "I'm sure that's supposed to be comforting, but it really isn't."

Ryan smiled apologetically. "The good part is that volcanoes often spew smoke and ash and all that stuff before they blow their tops ... or so I've been told. Since the Montagne Del Fuego, the 'mountain of fire,' hasn't done any of that, I've been told there's really nothing to be concerned about."

Maggie frowned. Scott put his arm around her and pulled her close to him.

"Don't worry, sweetie. I'll watch out for you." He kissed her on the top of her head. With his strong arms wrapped around her, she relaxed in his embrace.

Just hold me and I'll be fine.

He kissed her once more, released her, and took her by the hand. "Even earthquakes can't stop the work around here. Are you ready?"

He led her to the makeshift clinic, and they spent most of the morning setting things up in anticipation of the appointments to come. Although the next few days were busy, Maggie never lost sight of the upcoming holiday, due to the joyous anticipation and preparation among the people of Ryan's small congregation. Learning how to make tamales, arroz dulce, and champurrado endeared Maggie to the local women, and her efforts earned Scott's praise. The nearness of him during Christmastime was all she felt she needed to make their holiday complete.

Her first Christmas in Mexico exposed her to *La Posadas*, the nightly procession led by two children from mid-December until the night before Christmas, and this festive buildup delighted Maggie. She relished listening to the heartfelt songs of the season sung as the parade reenacted the journey of Mary and Joseph to Bethlehem. The night before Christmas culminated with a church service and Ryan's message of God's love and hope for the world manifested through the birth of a tiny baby born nearly two thousand years ago.

Relaxing in a plane headed back to the City of Angels, Maggie glanced over at Scott, who sat with his eyes closed, an open Bible in his lap. His breathing was regular and rhythmic.

How in the world can you sleep in that seat?

She smiled as she closed his Bible. Before placing it in the seatback pocket, her finger traced his name imprinted in gold at the bottom of the black cover. Maggie rested her head against the back of her seat.

I can't believe we did so much while we were there. We vaccinated over 100 children! So many of them could have died without those vaccines. Scott was so right. I feel so wonderful inside … teaching those moms how to take care of their children, and those two we're getting the cleft palate repairs done for nothing … this has been an amazing trip!

She smiled at Scott as he shuffled in the seat. His long, lanky frame seemed cramped in the small seat, but his deep breathing told Maggie that he was in a well-deserved slumber. She placed her hand on his.

You kept your word, Scott. This trip, the time I spent with you, even the midnight texting ... it was really wonderful. I can't wait until we go again. I wish we could have spent more time alone, but at least we were together. This was the best Christmas I've had in a long time, and it was all because of you. She looked over at him one more time, smiled, and then closed her eyes and fell into a sweet sleep.

CHAPTER FOUR

THEIR WEDDING WAS simple, yet elegant, in a small chapel overlooking the Pacific Ocean. Ryan had agreed to fly to Los Angeles to officiate the ceremony. Tears filled Maggie's eyes as she listened to him speak about love and the covenant of marriage. He wove the concept of matrimonial love into the overall plan of love that God had for all mankind. As he talked about the responsibilities of husband and wife, Ryan likened their roles to the relationship between Jesus and the Church, and when he prompted, Maggie looked once again into the deep blue eyes of Scott Devereaux and promised to love and cherish him forever. The joy she felt was unspeakable as she listened while Scott repeated similar vows to those she had just spoken.

Taking her into his arms, Scott kissed her softly, and the small gathering of family and friends applauded happily as Ryan pronounced Scott and Maggie husband and wife. Before releasing her, Scott whispered in her ear, "You have made me the happiest man on earth, Mrs. Devereaux."

Maggie gazed intently upon the face of her husband, memorizing the moment.

I love you, Scott, with all my heart, and I always will. With you by my side, nothing could be more perfect. All she could see was unconditional love and the promise of a bright tomorrow.

Their two-week Mexican honeymoon gave Maggie and Scott the opportunity to see more of the tropical country than they had seen in Santa Molina. During the first half of their blissful vacation, they stayed in a resort on the Yucatan peninsula, enjoying the newness of being husband and wife. Following the recommendation of the concierge, they took an inland tour through Mayan country and explored the ancient ruins of the Mesoamerican civilization, while sampling much of the local cuisine in the Cancún area.

As their trip was approaching its final days, they relaxed in a cabin on the shores of Lake Yaotl. Sweet serenity enveloped the first hint of the summer evening as the last trace of golden sunlight slowly disappeared below the western horizon, leaving a fading shimmering path on the rippling surface of the lake. Hues of pink and orange spread across the twilight sky as a lone heron sailed above the glistening water, searching for its last meal before settling down for the night.

Maggie sat quietly on the wooden steps of the patio leading from the small cabin to the sandy shore of the lake below. She relished the soft caress of the warm July breeze and breathed in the aroma of her new husband's cooking; he claimed to be preparing the best-tasting steaks in all of Mexico.

She turned to meet the love-filled gaze of the man who had captured her heart nearly one year ago. With only a hint of grey at his temples, Maggie swooned over how handsome her thirty-five year old husband was. Wearing an open Guayabara shirt that she had insisted on buying at a local souvenir shop, Scott mouthed, "I love you," then returned to his grilling.

Five minutes later he announced, "Dinner is served, sweetheart," and removed the steaks with a dramatic flair.

"Smells absolutely divine," stated Maggie as she stood to inspect the meal. She rubbed her finger across the top of one steak and touched the tip of her finger to her tongue. "Hmmm … this tastes delicious!"

Scott bowed slightly as he set their food on the patio table. Turning toward Maggie, he quickly took her into his arms and kissed her. "Yes, it does!" Maggie hugged her husband once more and kissed him forcefully on the lips. "I was talking about the steak."

Scott feigned surprise. "Oh, you were?" He sat beside her and took her hand in his as they both bowed their heads, and he prayed.

"I am so glad we decided to come here for our honeymoon. This lake is beautiful, and, well, it's perfect. And then, to know we get to spend a few days with Ryan … I am … so happy!" Maggie's voice broke as she looked longingly at her husband. "I love you so much."

"I love you too, sweetheart. My life couldn't be more perfect than it is now!"

The next few days passed quickly, and when Maggie and Scott arrived at Ryan's church, the locals were overjoyed at seeing them again. They insisted upon throwing a traditional

Mexican fiesta celebrating their wedding. Decorations of red, orange, and yellow hung from the trees in the courtyard of the church, and strolling musicians added to the atmosphere of celebration. Terra cotta pots filled with zinnias, white daisies, and lavender orchids added a touch of floral festivity. Tacos, enchiladas, burritos, and tamales of various types were laid out on platters. Punchbowls, filled with various fruit juices, had floating flowers in them.

Overwhelmed by the outpouring of love, tears frequently pooled in Maggie's eyes as the well-wishers hugged and, in halting English, congratulated her. As the celebration continued, Maggie would often see Scott watching her from afar as he, too, received hearty congratulations from the people of this small community. Each time Scott's gaze met hers, Maggie felt more happiness than she thought possible.

Later that evening, as Maggie lay in the arms of her husband, listening to the sounds of the night, she thanked God for the wonderful man He had given to her, and the many blessings in her life. She vowed to get to know Him better, and perhaps someday have a relationship with God in the way that Scott and Ryan had. She knew that would please Scott immensely, and decided she would make a concerted effort to talk to Ryan about that before she and Scott flew home.

The next day began early. A flock of green parrots flew overhead, squawking as they passed by. Maggie stopped and looked up, and then headed for the two-story structure that housed the dining room. The smell of cooked bacon wafted into the courtyard, and as she strolled toward the dining hall, Ryan walked over to join her.

"Good morning, Sister. May I join you for breakfast? I saw Scotty heading that way earlier."

Maggie smiled at her brother-in-law. "Indeed you may. It's a beautiful day, isn't it?"

Ryan nodded. "Seems like they've all been that way recently." He turned to her and took her hands. "Maggie, I am so happy to have you in our family."

"Thank you, Ryan. That means so much to me. I was wondering …" She took a deep breath. "I know how important God is to you … and Scott. I've seen how you both live your lives according to your faith, and I … I want to understand your faith, and I want to be part of your family in every way. Before we leave for Los Angeles … could you and I talk?"

Ryan had been praying fervently for Maggie ever since Scott had confided to Ryan that he intended to marry her.

Thank you, Lord. Please let your Spirit guide my words when we talk. Open her heart to you, Lord.

While Ryan knew the potential pitfalls of a marriage between a believer and non-believer, he had chosen his words carefully when speaking to his brother about his decision to marry before Maggie surrendered her life to God. Scott, however, had been very confident that she would come to know the Lord as her Savior, and together they would serve Him in the medical field. While their impending marriage had troubled Ryan, he had kept it between himself and God, praying earnestly for Maggie's salvation. Today, it seemed, might be that day, and Ryan struggled to contain his joy.

"Of course, Maggie, I would be happy to talk with you about that. Maybe tonight?"

Maggie nodded, and Ryan noted that her face visibly relaxed. "That would be great. Could Scott be there?"

"Absolutely! I know he'd love that."

The chiming of Maggie's cell phone interrupted their conversation. She smiled at Ryan as she pulled her phone from her pants pocket. "I'm sure that's Scott wondering where I am." She looked at the message. "Yes, it's from him."

Suddenly, the ground began to shake. Maggie lost her balance, and Ryan grabbed her arm as they both were thrown to the ground. As the intensity of the quake grew, two cabins lost their support system and crashed to the ground. Ryan protectively held Maggie, and they remained crouched in the courtyard for the duration of the earthquake. Twenty-three seconds later, the seismic activity stopped, and the dust began to settle. Screams and crying from trapped people began to fill the air.

"You OK?" asked Ryan as they staggered to their feet.

Maggie nodded as she turned toward the dining hall. The once two-story building was now a massive pile of broken timbers and cracked cement.

"Scott! Scott!" Maggie screamed hysterically as she ran toward the dining room. Clawing at the rubble, she desperately tried to move massive blocks of broken cement. Her fingernails tore, and her fingertips bled as she frantically tried to get to Scott.

Please, God, let him be OK!

Tears streamed down Maggie's face as her frustration level rose; she could not move the huge chunks of concrete. Suddenly, her cell phone chimed. Maggie fumbled for her phone and flipped open the screen. It was a text from Scott!

'r u OK?'

He's alive!

Maggie typed as fast as she could. '*Yes. You?*' She waited expectantly for his reply.

In seconds, her phone chimed again. *'ok cant move much'*

Maggie willed herself to remain calm, but her fingers shook as she tried to hit the letters on the keyboard. She looked around for Ryan, but he was busy orchestrating the rescuers.

'Help coming.'

She continued to dig at the rubble until she felt a strong hand on her shoulder. She turned and found herself looking into Ryan's worried face.

"Maggie, I'm sorry … but, we could really use your help with the injured. I've got men working here. We'll get him out."

Maggie gazed around her and a gasp escaped her lips as she surveyed the damaged compound. She reluctantly surrendered the job of search and rescue to the local men and allowed her medical training to take over. Tucking her phone securely in her pocket, she began to triage the injured for treatment priority. As the hours passed, she tended the wounded while texting Scott as often as she could.

Early in the afternoon, the first casualty was pulled from the wreckage of the dining room. It was one of the women who had taught Maggie how to make tamales on her first visit.

No! Not her … not Julia!

No matter how hard Maggie tried, she couldn't stop the tears. She felt for her phone, her lifeline to Scott, and pulled it out of her pocket.

'How are you doing?' she texted, then waited … and waited.

'ok tired.'

Maggie felt panic rise in her.

You can't die! Fear gripped her fingers and she tried to text quickly, but it took several attempts before she could get the message correct. Through her tears, she finally managed to type '*We're almost there.*'

Five minutes passed before her phone chimed again. "*luv u so much.*'

Maggie frantically tried to type. '*I love you too. Hold on.*' She pressed "send" and stared at her phone, waiting for Scott's reply.

None came.

Exactly how much time passed before Maggie saw a silhouette move toward her in the shadows of twilight, she did not know, but when Ryan emerged in the dim light of the main building, the look on his face told her that Scott was gone.

PART TWO

THREE YEARS LATER

CHAPTER FIVE

"I REALLY AM fine," protested Colin Grant as the paramedics lifted his gurney into the ambulance. "This is a little ridiculous, don't you think, Gary? I feel fine."

The older man turned from the paramedics to address the young man on the gurney and ran his hand through his salt and pepper hair. "Last time I checked you were an entertainer, not a doctor, right? They don't tell you how to sing, you don't tell them how to practice medicine. Besides, this won't take very long." Gary Petty turned back to the paramedic recording Colin's information and began to give explicit instructions regarding his expectations of the singer's treatment.

Colin sighed in resignation.

Emergency … great … this is going to take forever.

With only a few cuts left to finish the album, Colin was anxious to complete the work. He wanted to return to his home in England for the Easter season, but that wouldn't happen until his part of the album was complete.

The paramedic, entering through the rear of the ambulance, interrupted Colin's thoughts. He adjusted the intravenous drip, made a few notations on a clipboard, and then asked Colin how he felt.

"*Fine.*" He stared at Gary standing outside the ambulance door and emphasized, "I don't think this is really necessary."

"You need to calm down, Colin. Getting upset won't help your blood pressure," said Gary, his hands on his hips.

Colin started to cross his arms, but was hindered by the IV line. "My blood pressure? Nothing's wrong with my blood pressure. And what makes you think I'm upset?" He dropped his hands down by his side.

"Well, to begin with, that British accent of yours becomes much more pronounced when you're irritated. You're also throwing your hands down in disgust."

The paramedic re-inflated the blood pressure cuff and placed his stethoscope in position. "Well, since we're already here, Mr. Grant, it won't hurt to let us and the docs at Eastmont check you out."

"Fine." Colin resigned himself to the ER visit as his blood pressure was taken. "You know, it's got to be high." He watched the paramedic write some notes again and wondered if the findings were within normal limits.

No matter. Gary's going to make sure I have a complete physical exam, and he'll tell me I need a clean bill of health before I get back to recording. He winced as he moved his arm, tugging on the IV line. *Sometimes managers are more trouble than they're worth.* He exhaled slowly. *What am I thinking? Gary's only looking out for me. I'm sorry, Lord. Forgive me.*

Colin reflected on how Gary had guided his career, quite successfully, over the years, and had, in fact, become somewhat of a surrogate father to him. Gary had believed in Colin when no one would take the time to listen to a demo tape from the inexperienced singer with the boyish good looks and enthusiastic demeanor. Gary's persistence had led to an audition with one of the biggest recording companies in the entertainment industry, which resulted in Colin's first recording contract. His unique style of singing, coupled with his incredible vocal range, led to a string of number one hits on the popular music charts, making him a favorite with those in the young to mid-adult demographic range.

"Forgive me, Lord," he whispered. Sighing once more, he turned his attention to the dripping of the intravenous fluid and found solace in the steady rhythm of the liquid. He closed his eyes and allowed his thoughts to drift back to the earlier events of the day.

Often starting his day early with an exhilarating run along the almost empty beach, Colin relished the time alone. While he ran, he often generated new ideas for songs, frequently humming the new melodies, and then writing them down upon his return home. More importantly, Colin used the time to meditate on his morning devotions, to pray and seek God's guidance for the day; he coveted the early morning conversations he had with the Lord. The rhythmic pounding of the waves over the shore enveloped him with a calmness of spirit and gave him time to reflect upon the Scriptures he had read upon rising, as well as an opportunity to talk to his Savior.

This particular morning he focused his thinking on the path that led him to his current status. He fondly remembered the years he spent singing in his church choir as a young boy, and the smiling faces of his parents and brothers watching him from the congregation. Church was the focal point of his young life until a drunk driver speeding the wrong way on a thoroughfare robbed him of his parents and his tender faith. He wasn't angry or bitter toward God; he had simply lost the impetus for continuing the religious part of his life.

After the death of his parents, his two older brothers, Josh and Kurt, quickly filled the void created. Respectively eight and six years older than Colin, they were his guiding light through his teen years, and encouraged him to follow his heart when it came to deciding about a career in music. Colin took their advice, and, after completing his undergraduate degree, he moved to New York City. In less than two years, he signed a multimillion dollar recording contract that opened the door to a promising career in entertainment. He always believed in his heart that his parents would have been proud of his decisions, and his successes.

However, despite his accomplishments in the music world, Colin felt that his life still was missing something very important. It was the return to his spiritual roots in the summer of his twenty-sixth year that brought him the fulfillment he had been seeking. Taking a brief hiatus from singing, he had returned to his family home for what he hoped to be a time of relaxation and personal reflection. On impulse, Colin had visited his parents' old church, and there he had met the current pastor. Initially hesitant to share his feelings, Colin found the friendly demeanor of the pastor easy to respond to, and shared his fears and frustrations about the emptiness he felt in his life.

Colin began to attend services on a fairly regular basis during that summer, finding the people kind, friendly, and sincere in their faith. Several of the older members remembered his mother and father. He never tired of hearing about things his parents had done at the church, and began to understand what it meant to put one's faith to work.

During the services, he listened intently to the pastor's messages, and the many verses he memorized as a young boy came back to him with new meaning. At home, he found his mother's Bible and began to study some of the passages she had underlined. It gave him great joy when he found certain verses she had circled and written her sons' names beside them. Colin continued his meetings with the pastor, and after a series of shared conversations, he realized that, although he had accepted Christ as his Savior as a young boy, he was missing a personal relationship with the Lord. Near the end of that summer, in the quiet of the pastor's study, Colin surrendered his life to God.

Shifting his musical focus from contemporary pop to gospel had stunned the music world, but Colin deeply believed that the genre change in his career was part of God's perfect plan for his life. Although his popularity waned slightly, he never regretted the decision to shift his focus. His loyal fan base from earlier days continued to buy his CDs, no matter the type, and Colin believed God would use his music to spread the gospel message of hope, love, and salvation through Christ.

In the morning, as the sun had begun to peak over the southern California mountains, Colin was finishing his run along the sandy shore of the Malibu coast when he felt the first twinge in his chest. He paid little heed to it since it quickly disappeared. Climbing the steps from the beach to his patio, a sharper pain radiated across Colin's chest to his left shoulder. Stopping for a moment to grab the stair railing, he winced as he took another deep breath. He breathed out slowly to minimize the discomfort, and although the pain dissipated almost immediately, it was not so fast as to escape notice from Gary, who had just walked out onto the patio.

"Something wrong?" Gary asked, frowning slightly.

Colin shook his head. "No, just some muscle aches, I guess." He looked at Gary, then grinned. "I know what you're thinking. It is not a heart attack." He grabbed an apple off the patio table and took a bite.

"Everyone who has a heart attack denies it," Gary cautioned, crossing his arms. "Maybe we should call someone."

"Do I look like I'm having a heart attack? Besides, I'm only twenty-nine. You need to worry about you, old man!" He laughed as he headed inside to prepare for the day's work.

Later that day at the studio, Colin took his place at a piano, and the small group of musicians warmed up by playing and singing a few favorite hymns. The recording session was going very well until another sharp pain prompted Colin to ask for a short break. He stood up and pushed the microphone away.

"You all right, Colin?"

Colin glanced toward the glass window and nodded, "Yeah, just a little tired, I guess. Let's break for lunch, OK?"

"Good timing; lunch just arrived," said Gary as Colin exited the sound booth. His worried eyes followed Colin.

"I'm sorry, Gary. I don't mean to worry you. Really, I think I'm just tired." Colin sat down to a ham and turkey hoagie and a soda.

"It's my job to worry about you, kid. You're my bread and butter." Gary shook his head. He then inspected his pastrami sandwich before taking a big bite. "Having any other symptoms?"

"You mean besides the shortness of breath and pain radiating up and down my left arm?" Colin replied without looking up at Gary.

Gary looked up in alarm, mid-bite.

Colin grinned broadly. "I'm just kidding you. I'm fine, really. Probably just heartburn or something like that."

Gary swallowed his bite. "Would you tell me if it was something more?"

"Probably not, but really, I'm good. Y'know, we had that volleyball game Saturday night. Maybe I pulled a muscle." He took another sip of soda.

The rest of the recording session was uneventful until the day's last cut. As Colin reached forward to move a piece of sheet music, a jolt of pain made him pull his arm back quickly, initiating a muted "Ow!" from the singer.

"That's it, Colin. I'm calling for medical help," Gary declared.

"What? Why? I'm telling you it is just a pulled muscle." Gary met Colin's shocked expression with steel eyes. Colin frowned, but said nothing.

A bump in the road brought Colin back to the present. He opened his eyes and frowned.

"You doing OK, Mr. Grant?"

"Yeah. Just wondering how I'm going to apologize to my manager." Colin watched as the paramedic regulated the flow of the intravenous solution. "I also want to apologize to you for my behavior earlier. I didn't mean to take it out on you."

The paramedic smiled as he adjusted Colin's oxygen mask. "No need, sir. My boss can be rather insistent, too, so I totally understand the frustrations."

"I suppose it is better to be safe than sorry. Besides, God has His reasons for allowing things like this to happen.

I wish I wasn't so stubborn and could quit fighting Him when they do."

The paramedic nodded. "Yeah, I know what you mean. Sometimes the Lord has to knock me in the head a few times before I even realize He's knocking."

"You're a Christian?"

"Yes, sir, since I was a kid. My folks always took me to church, and I got saved when I was six years old." He laughed lightly. "Had no choice ... my granddaddy was the preacher, my daddy was a deacon, and my mama was my Sunday school teacher. But all kidding aside, I try to serve Him the best I can in my job. Can't imagine living without Him."

Colin extended his hand to shake that of the young man's. "I'm happy to meet you."

"It's an honor, sir. I've got most of your CDs, before and after. I really admire the stand you took for your faith."

Colin felt humbled before the young paramedic. "I'm sorry it took me so long to find my way back to Him, but I am very grateful that He has allowed me to continue doing what I love for Him."

"Kind of like the prodigal?"

"Yeah, and let me tell you, it sure was good to come home!"

The thirty-minute ride to Eastmont Hospital was without incident, and as the paramedic helped the nurse move Colin to the exam table in the ER, he looked at the singer promising, "I'll be praying for you, brother." They shook hands once again, and Colin watched him leave the room. He quietly asked God one more time to forgive him for being so difficult with Gary, and then asked the Lord to bless the young paramedic whose encouraging words had warmed his heart and touched his soul.

CHAPTER SIX

"YOU'RE GOING TO be just fine," said Valerie Garrett as she ruffled the hair of the eight-year-old boy sitting on the examination table. "Once that cast is on, you'll be invincible, like Superman!" The slender emergency room nurse smiled at the young freckle-faced lad, then turned to his worried mother. "They'll be coming for you in just a bit to get the cast put on. You can go with him. When they're finished, they'll send you back here. See me before you go, OK?"

The mother nodded and wiped her tears. "Thank you so much. I was so scared when he fell off the bunk bed."

Valerie patted the mother's hand. "Accidents happen all the time, especially to little boys. We'll probably see a lot more of you in the next few years!" Wiping a strand of hair from in front of her eyes, Valerie scanned the waiting area as she left the treatment room.

This is going to be a long night.

Walking into the triage center, she noticed a group of nurses huddled together, whispering.

"What's going on?" Valerie asked as she wrote the letters O-R-T-H on the white board, indicating that her young patient was headed to orthopedics for a cast.

"You'll never guess who just arrived in treatment room four," replied a young red-haired desk clerk, handing her a blank chart.

"Who?" asked Valerie, taking the chart and heading toward the patient in question.

"Colin Grant."

Valerie stopped and turned abruptly. "The singer?" Her eyes widened as the three women nodded in unison.

The night just got more interesting.

"Hmm … page Dr. Devereaux. I think we had better make sure he gets the best doctor we have. You never know if there's going to be a publicist or paparazzi around. Can't afford to make any mistakes with this one."

Within seconds, the P.A. system beckoned Dr. Maggie Devereaux to the emergency room.

Valerie entered the treatment room to find several people circled around the hospital bed. Unable to see the patient, Valerie cleared her throat to get their attention.

"Excuse me," Valerie said, firmly.

Gary Petty turned around. "Oh, I'm sorry miss. Can I help you?"

Valerie's eyes narrowed; her lips set in a firm line.

He must be in charge, or at least he thinks he is.

"I need to speak with the patient privately; everyone needs to leave the room. You can wait in—"

"I am staying here with him," said Gary, his arms folded across his chest.

"Excuse me?"

Gary politely, but firmly, restated his position. "I am his manager, and I must stay with him."

A new voice penetrated the tension in the room.

"No, you won't. Nurse Garrett has asked you to leave. You and your acquaintances will wait in the waiting room—now."

Everyone's head turned, including Valerie's. A hint of a smile crossed her lips.

That's my sister-in-law. Get 'em, Maggie!

Maggie leaned on the door frame, her arms folded across her chest. Valerie shook her head knowingly.

Poor guy. I wouldn't want to be on the receiving end of her icy stare.

She stepped back slightly to allow the men to see Maggie clearly.

Gary hesitated a moment. "Fine, we'll wait outside. I assume you'll let me know when we can come back in?" Receiving no answer, he turned back to Colin and whispered, "I'll be right out there if you need me."

Colin shook his head. "I'll be fine, Gary. Really. I think I'm going to be in very good hands. You said I'd get the best care here, right?"

Gary nodded as he moved toward the doctor standing in the doorway. "I'm Gary Petty, Colin's manager." He held out a card; Maggie didn't take it. Gary cleared his throat, then set the card on the bedside table. "If you need anything, please let me know. Take good care of him."

The commanding doctor stared sternly at the manager. "We take good care of *everyone* here, Mr. Petty." She made no effort to move until everyone had maneuvered past her.

As Valerie began taking vital signs and making notations on the chart, Maggie walked toward Colin. He shifted in the bed, keeping his eyes on the doctor as she crossed the room.

"I'm Dr. Devereaux. What brings you here, Mr. Grant?" asked Maggie, her arms still crossed over her chest.

"Chest pain … well, probably muscle pain, but Gary is a worrier and he—"

"Why do you think it's muscular pain?" Maggie removed her stethoscope from a pocket in her lab coat.

"I played volleyball Saturday night. It became pretty competitive. I just figured I pulled something."

"Where is the pain located?"

"Around here," he said, indicating his central chest area.

"Have you been sick lately?"

"No, not really. I had a cold a couple of weeks ago, I guess, but nothing serious."

His eyes locked on her face as she put the stethoscope to his chest.

"It kind of goes away when I lean forward," said Colin.

"I see."

"You see?"

"Mr. Grant, would you sit up for me?" asked Maggie while straightening up to allow Colin room to rise.

He pushed himself up, and leaned forward. He also obeyed all her commands to breathe deeply, to follow her fingers as they moved in front of his face, and to open his mouth as she looked inside. Maggie tapped on his chest and back, and then listened again to his heart. She made several notations on the chart, and then spoke with the nurse before turning back to him.

"What do all those letters mean?" asked Colin, after Maggie ordered a CBC, ABG, and EKG.

"Well, Mr. Grant, I am going to order some blood work and a couple of preliminary heart tests for a baseline. You'll also have a chest x-ray. I'll know more once I get those test results."

"Do you really think it could be my heart?"

"I really can't say at this time. I'll be better able to answer your questions after I get the results back on your tests. Nurse Garrett will get a history from you and that will help, but really, until I have a little more information, any diagnosis would be purely conjecture at this time."

"Conjecture works good if it's positive."

Maggie frowned. "Let's wait for the test results, Mr. Grant." She handed the chart to Valerie. "Keep him on oxygen for now, and let me know when the results are back."

Valerie nodded her acknowledgement and placed the oxygen mask on Colin's face.

He watched Maggie walk out of the room, and then turned his attention to Valerie. "Wow, she's not someone I'd want to cross. Is she a good doctor?"

"The best," Valerie responded confidently before asking Colin a few more questions for his admittance forms. Upon completion, she asked, "Would you like me to send in one of your friends?"

"I suppose I should say yes, but in reality, it's nice to just lay here in the quiet and not have someone hovering over me. Not that I don't appreciate all they do, it's just that sometimes they worry a little too much."

"I guess that comes with the territory."

"Yes, it does. And I'm being terribly ungrateful, aren't I? I suppose I should talk to Gary. He'll be worried sick if I don't tell him something. Would you mind asking him to come back in, I would really appreciate that. He's the older guy, my manager."

"I figured as much. How about I give him a time limit?"

"That'd be great."

He lay back against the pillow, readjusted the oxygen mask, and closed his eyes. After taking a deep breath, he exhaled slowly. Within minutes, his breathing became rhythmic and steady as sleep overcame him.

"How are you feeling?"

Roused from the haze of light slumber, Colin slowly opened his eyes and saw the concerned face of his manager. He looked down at the translucent green mask on his face and touched it with his hand. His eyes darted around the room before answering.

"Uh … I think I'm doing pretty good." He pulled his athletic, six-foot frame up a bit on the bed. "They're running some tests, and then the doctor said she'd know something later." He ran his fingers through his blonde hair. "Relax, I promise you, I am not going to die."

Gary sighed as he pulled up a chair. "I'll feel a lot better when I know it's not your heart."

"How many guys my age have heart attacks?"

"That is not the point."

"The point is you're trying to take care of a stubborn young man who is too preoccupied with himself to notice and be grateful." Colin looked directly at Gary and smiled, his cheeks burning. "And for that, I am very appreciative." Gary visibly relaxed in the chair, and Colin realized how much strain Gary had been under in the last few hours. "And I'm sorry."

"There's nothing to be sorry for, Colin. I'm just glad you finally listened to me."

"I always listen to you."

Gary snickered.

"What? Don't I always listen to you? Well, no matter. It could be worse. I'm in a nice, if somewhat small, bed. I have beautiful women taking care of me. I get all the oxygen I can breathe, and a non-stop drink." He nodded toward the intravenous solution dripping into his vein. "What more could a guy want?" Both men chuckled, and Colin was glad the awkward manager-client moment had shifted back to their more comfortable friend-friend relationship.

"I'll postpone the rest of the session until you're up and about, so don't worry about that. Everyone will be glad to take a bit of time off and hit the beach, but they are sending you their thoughts and prayers," said Gary. He fiddled with the bed controls. "Do you think you should get some sleep?"

"Wasn't that what I was doing?"

Gary frowned.

"OK, OK. Besides, if I say 'no,' you'll tell me I need it, so I may as well give up and close my eyes."

Gary stood up, and moved the chair back to its original spot. "I better go before Attila the Hun comes back and orders me out again. I'll tell the others that you're resting comfortably, and send them home to get some shuteye, but I'll be here in the waiting room until we get some news about what's going on with you." He left Colin just as a lab tech entered to draw blood.

Several other hospital technicians came in for additional tests before Colin had another chance to close his eyes. Finally, after the last test was completed, Colin fell asleep to the dull sounds of the cardiac monitor at his bedside.

The nurses' station was buzzing with excitement as Maggie walked over to Valerie and the other members of the emergency room staff.

"What's going on?" she asked as she picked up Colin's chart to check his latest lab test results.

The nurses looked at Maggie incredulously.

"What's going on?" asked Traci, a registry nurse filling in for the evening. "Don't tell me you don't know who *he* is."

"Who? Mr. Grant?" Maggie mentally interpreted Colin's blood tests.

Valerie stepped in to rescue her sister-in-law. "Yes, Dr. D. That's Colin Grant, the singer."

"Really? What does he sing?" Maggie sat down on a stool next to the chart stand, pulled one out, and began writing.

Several of the nurses rolled their eyes and murmured among themselves.

"What?" Maggie asked without looking up. "I don't exactly keep up with today's music."

"He's probably the most popular singer of the decade," retorted the desk clerk. "You know, popular soft rock. Well, he used to be. Now he sings gospel. Everyone loves him."

"Is that so? Well, if he's so popular, where are the fans that I've heard are always following celebrities everywhere they go?" Maggie placed her hand horizontally across her forehead, scanning the emergency room waiting area.

"Give them time," said Valerie. "As soon as the media gets wind of this, we'll be swarmed with fans and paparazzi. Even though he changed to religious stuff, I'll bet he's still got a tremendous amount of fans."

"Who cares what he sings," commented Traci. "He's great eye candy."

Maggie shook her head. "Oh, I get it now … there are fans here; they're just masquerading as nurses!" She chuckled at the ladies whose faces reddened slightly.

Valerie smiled. "You gotta admit Dr. D., he is good looking."

Maggie looked at her sister-in-law wide-eyed. "Valerie Garrett, you are married to my brother!"

Valerie giggled. "Yeah, the gate may be closed, but I can still look over the fence!"

Maggie rolled her eyes. "I am going to ignore that remark. I can only hope the rest of you will be able to focus on your work while he's here."

The clerk handed her another set of lab results. Maggie frowned as she studied the figures on the paper. "Especially since he won't be leaving us right away." She gave the lab results to Valerie, who perused them before attaching them to Colin's file.

"What if his manager wants to take him home?" asked another nurse.

"His manager doesn't make that decision. I do." Maggie stood up and headed toward Colin's room, leaving the women murmuring among themselves again.

Entering the room, Maggie saw that Colin's eyes were closed. She glanced up at the cardiac monitor before speaking.

"Mr. Grant," she said quietly.

Colin blinked his eyes open. "Hey, Doc. Do … you have my test … results?"

"Yes. First the good news—"

"There's bad news?" Colin's eyes popped open.

Calm him down, Maggie. He looks pretty scared.

"Yes, but not as bad as it could be. First of all, no heart attack. However, there's a strong possibility you have a condition known as pericarditis. Also, you are a bit dehydrated, and could probably use some sleep."

Colin pushed himself up, so his weight was on his elbows. "What's the pericarditis thing? Is that bad? Is that what caused the pain?"

"It's an inflammation of the membrane that surrounds the heart, however, it—"

"It really is my heart?"

A slight smile creased Maggie's lips. "Not actually. It's the lining *around* your heart. It—"

"What caused it?"

"That I can't tell you just yet, however—"

"Is it … I mean, will I—"

If you'd just let me finish a sentence!

"Mr. Grant, *you will get well.* You need to calm down and listen to me." She stood near the edge of the bed and softened her approach. "I want to keep you here for observation for another day or two. We'll treat you with some anti-inflammatories, take a few more tests, and make sure things are on the mend before we release you." She waited for him to interrupt her again. "You will still need the IV and the oxygen. Any questions?"

"So I'll live?" he asked with a crooked grin.

"Yes, you'll live." Maggie smiled. "Try not to worry too much. You'll be fine. I promise." She stood and turned to leave.

Colin sat up straight. "Are you going to be my doctor?"

Maggie turned back to him. "No, we'll be moving you upstairs to a private room to continue your care. I'll assign your case to a cardiologist on staff unless you have one of your own I can call."

Colin nodded as she turned to leave. "Hey, Doc?"

Maggie turned around again.

"No way I can keep you?"

Maggie shook her head. "No. You'll do much better with a doctor that specializes in heart issues."

Colin frowned. "Never hurts to ask."

"We'll move you as soon as a room is ready. If you need anything, just press that." She indicated the call button, then left the room.

Colin sighed as he watched Maggie leave. Within a few minutes, Gary rushed into the room.

"Colin, you OK? The doctor said I could come in, but she wouldn't tell me anything, except you have to stay. What's wrong?"

"She says it's pericarditis. The lining around my heart is inflamed, but she said I'd be fine with rest and meds."

"I can't believe it! How'd this happen? I just can't believe it."

"Hey, God's in control, remember? I'll be fine. Besides," Colin winked, "He sure sent me a gorgeous doctor, didn't He?"

After two days in a telemetry unit, the cardiologist declared Colin well enough for discharge. Despite Gary's best efforts, word did leak out to the press that Colin was in the hospital, and the medical center's spokesperson found it necessary to hold a press conference reassuring the media that Colin was doing well and would soon be released. Maintaining confidentiality regarding the actual medical reasons for his hospitalization, the spokesperson assuaged any fears the public held regarding the singer's health.

Emerging from the hospital in a wheelchair, despite his insistence that it was not necessary, Colin waved good-naturedly at several celebrity-based magazine photographers who waited at the hospital exit to snap pictures of the official discharge.

"How are you feeling, Colin?" called one of the photographers.

"Great! God's been good, and everyone here has been fantastic. I really appreciate all your prayers."

"When will you get back to recording?"

"As soon as Mr. Petty will let me." He patted Gary's hand, who shook his head as he wheeled Colin toward the car. Peppered with additional questions, Colin easily answered them all before Gary intervened.

"That's all for now, boys," he said and waved his hand. He held the door open as Colin moved into the front passenger seat of the car. Shutting the door, he walked to the opposite side of the car.

"I am glad this is over," Gary said, moving into the driver's seat.

"What? The paparazzi interrogation? At least they haven't forgotten me." Colin laid his head back on the leather headrest and closed his eyes.

"No. The whole hospitalization thing. I still think they should've been able to tell you more about this pericarditis. How can you have something this serious, and they not know what caused it?"

Colin glanced at Gary. "I guess we're not meant to know everything. Besides, as long as it's resolved, that's the most important part, don't you agree?"

"I suppose so. I guess God has it covered, huh?"

"He always does."

Three days later, Colin returned to the emergency room and found Valerie behind the nurses' station. It was just after eight A.M., and the waiting area was uncharacteristically empty. He slipped up to the counter and stood quietly, watching her write in a chart.

Sensing someone's presence, Valerie looked up.

Colin grinned. "Remember me?" He pushed his sunglasses up on his head.

Valerie's eyes lit up. "Of course I remember you, Mr. Grant. How can I help you? Is everything alright?"

"Yes, I'm fine. I was wondering if Dr. Devereaux was around."

Maggie? Why does he need to see Maggie? Valerie fought against her desire to interrogate Colin. "She's in with a patient. Is there something I can help you with?"

"Maybe ... I was wondering what you could tell me about her."

Valerie raised an eyebrow.

Really? What in the world does he want to know about Maggie?

Colin glanced around and grinned sheepishly. "I suppose the obvious question would be whether or not she is married."

Her mouth dropped open, but quickly closed as she attempted to recover her demeanor. She didn't know whether or not she should be answering his questions. "No ... no, she's not married."

Colin continued in a whisper. "I suppose she doesn't date patients?"

Valerie stared at Colin in disbelief. "I don't think so."

"Do you think she would have dinner with me ... as a sort of thank you?"

You want to have dinner with my sister-in-law? Oh my word! Colin Grant wants to have dinner with my sister-in-law! This is so awesome!

Quickly composing her thoughts, she heard herself say, "She's with a patient right now. Would you like to wait for her?"

"If you don't think she would mind, then yes, I would."

Twenty minutes passed by the time Maggie finished her examination of a very pregnant woman. Reassured that she was not in active labor, the woman left the hospital disappointed that her baby was not yet ready to be born. As Maggie came out to the nurse's station, she noticed Colin leaning on the counter talking with Valerie.

What's he doing here? Hmm ... he really is quite nice looking.

She steadied her gaze on his face and noticed his easy smile and relaxed manner as he spoke with Valerie. He straightened up immediately when Maggie entered the area.

"Dr. Devereaux, Mr. Grant would like a word with you," said Valerie as she nodded to Colin. "Good luck," she whispered to him as she headed toward the staff lounge. Colin grinned at Valerie.

"Mr. Grant? Is everything alright?" asked Maggie as she replaced the chart into its holder.

"No problem, Doc." Colin cleared his throat. "I was wondering if ... no, let me start over. I know you probably don't date patients, but I would like to thank you for ... no, that's not right either."

He is going to ask me out! I can't believe this; he's going to ask me out!

Maggie motioned for him to follow her to a more private section of the waiting room.

When the two were fully alone, Colin took in a deep breath and said, "Would you consider having dinner with me? I'd like to thank you for all that you did for me."

Okay, Maggie, let the man down gently. There is no way you're going out with this guy, no matter how sweet he sounds, or how handsome he is.

"Mr. Grant, it's against hospital policy for doctors to date their patients—"

"Yeah, I figured that, but in reality, I'm not your patient." He removed his discharge paper from his shirt pocket and pointed to a spot on it. "Right here, it says I am going to be the patient of Dr. Eliot. So, once I was officially discharged from the ER, I believe we weren't doctor-patient anymore, right? And didn't you say that I didn't need to see you anymore?"

Maggie studied the man before her.

Well, you're certainly not what I thought a rock star would be like. Not too arrogant. Polite. Definitely good looking. Too bad you're my patient. I might almost be interested.

"Mr. Grant—"

"Colin."

Maggie hesitated. "You seem to have really prepared your case, Mr. Grant. I appreciate your offer, but I really can't."

"Why not? It's just a thank you."

"You don't need to thank me. I was doing my job." Maggie crossed her arms.

"Hmm, defensive posture. That's never a good sign. Hear me out, Doc, please. This is really just a thank you for not subjecting me to too many medical tests. You found the problem right away, and that deserves a thank you. Besides, you told me I should go out to dinner and relax." Colin spread out his hands in front of him.

He's persistent all right.

"First, I didn't do anything any other doctor would not have done. Second, I meant with your friends. Third, I don't date patients." Maggie pointed her index finger at him.

"Ever?"

"Ever."

"What if it were a year from now? Could you date me then?"

Maggie eyed him suspiciously. "Maybe."

"How about six months from now? Would that be long enough?"

"Possibly."

Colin crossed his arms and grinned. "How about one month from now?"

I know exactly where you're going with this, and it is not going to work!

Maggie started to speak, but Colin interjected.

"Aw, c'mon, Doc, you just admitted you could date a patient if the timing was right. We just have to find the right time interval. How 'bout it?"

Maggie shook her head, struggling with what to do and say next.

I need to just say no and walk away. He's a former patient, but he's so, so ... What am I thinking? There's absolutely no way. She stood up straight.

Colin spoke his next words very carefully. "I know that stance. You've made up your mind, but hear me out. I think I know what you're thinking. This guy is crazy. I don't know him; he doesn't know me. He's just some self-centered celebrity who is used to getting anything he wants, and now he wants to have dinner with me. I really would understand if you said no, but I was just hoping that maybe you'd say yes. It's just a dinner. Nothing more. I just want to thank you ... and maybe get to know you a little bit." He paused, and ran his fingers through his blonde hair.

"Another thing, you might as well know that if you agree, it would probably need to be at my place. I just want you to have all the facts before you totally turn me down."

Colin took a deep breath. "There's always the chance that if we go some place public, someone might snap a picture, and you could end up on the front page of some tabloid. I know you wouldn't want that, so if you come to my place, well, it's pretty private, and no photographers.

"We wouldn't really be alone though. Gary would be there, somewhere, but not with us. He lives at my house ... would you please have dinner with me?"

Maggie's head continued to wrestle with her heart. *If I say yes, I'm going against my professional principles. If I say no, well, I'm not too sure I want to say no. He really is quite nice, and dinner would probably be very interesting. What am I thinking? He's a famous singer. We have nothing in common.*

What will my nurses say? What will Valerie say? But he is very, very nice and ...

Just then, Gary Petty walked into the room.

"Are you ready, Colin?" he asked as he nodded at Maggie. "Can't thank you enough, Doc, for all you've done. I really appreciate it. I'll make sure he takes better care of himself."

Maggie noticed Colin shake his head slightly and frown. He looked at her and she wondered what thoughts lay behind his hopeful eyes.

I need to answer him.

"We're all set, right?" asked Gary. Neither Maggie nor Colin answered.

Colin looked at Maggie. Gary looked at Colin, then to Maggie, then back to Colin.

Maggie took a deep breath, and looked straight at Colin. "Alright," she said.

Colin stared at Maggie. "Alright? 'Alright' to me?"

Maggie nodded. She watched him carefully.

Colin repeated, "Yes?" Maggie watched as the questioning look on his face turned into one of delight.

She frowned for a moment. "I hope I don't regret this," she whispered.

"You won't, I promise," Colin whispered back. "When's a good night for you?"

Maggie thought for a moment. "How about next Thursday?"

"Thursday, it is!" Colin grinned as he wrote down his address, and handed her the paper.

"Hmm ... I wonder how much I could get for this information on eBay." She waved the paper in the air. Colin and Gary glanced at each other, then at Maggie.

Oh my goodness, they actually think I would do it.

"I'm just kidding. I promise I will not reproduce or share this information with *anyone*. Cross my heart." She drew an imaginary cross over the left pocket of her lab coat with her finger.

Both men visibly relaxed.

I wonder what it's like living like that. I can't imagine living in a fish bowl. I sure hope it wasn't a mistake accepting this invitation. Oh well, not much I can do about it now.

"I'll see you Thursday," Colin said.

When Maggie nodded, he and Gary said their goodbyes and left.

Maggie slowly walked into the staff lounge and poured a cup of coffee. Seeing that the room was empty, she exhaled deeply and sat at a table in the corner of the room. Nearing the midpoint of a twenty-four hour shift, her eyes were dry and heavy. Her mind wandered to her final conversation with Colin Grant.

"What am I thinking?" she murmured, "Why did I even agree to this?" Her thoughts turned to Scott, and she felt an intense emptiness in her heart.

Scott, what am I thinking?

She paused for a moment, then softly whispered, "And what in the world am I going to tell Valerie?"

CHAPTER SEVEN

Y OU'RE REALLY GOING out with him?" asked
Valerie, her eyes opened wide. "When did this happen? I mean, I know he wanted to ask you, but you
didn't say anything about it."

Maggie sat across from Valerie in the hospital cafeteria
playing with the lettuce in her chef salad. She put her fork
down and looked at her sister-in-law.

"I know, and to tell you the truth, I don't know why I
said I'd go. But I did. And now I'm stuck," grumbled Maggie.

"When is it?"

"Thursday night. I probably should go get a CD of his
after work today, so I know something about his music. I
don't want to appear totally ignorant of who he is."

"You can borrow one of mine. He's amazing to listen to.
I tell you, Maggie, he's quite a catch!"

"I am not looking for a catch," Maggie sat back and
crossed her arms. "I am going to *one* dinner at his place."

Valerie perked up. "His place? Oh, my goodness, I don't think I can take much more of this. Wait until I tell Will." She fanned her face with both of her hands.

"Valerie, you can't tell him. No one can know."

"Like, I'm going to keep it from him. He'll be thrilled. He'll think you've finally let something into your life besides medicine."

"It's one dinner," argued Maggie. "And it's not like I'm cloistered in this hospital."

"Really? I don't know why you even own that condo." She took a bite of her sandwich. "What are you wearing?"

Maggie shook her head. "Don't know. Haven't thought about it."

"You should." Valerie took another bite of her sandwich before continuing. "Something not 'doctory.' You know, don't dress like you're going to a medical convention."

Maggie shook her head, then sipped her coffee. "I hope I'm not making a mistake."

"A mistake? How could it be a mistake?"

"Well," began Maggie, "I don't want this to seem like something it's not. I mean, he just wants to say 'thank you,' that's all. I'm probably just being ridiculous." She stopped again, choosing her words carefully. "It is *not* a date."

Valerie reached across the table and took Maggie's hand in her own. "It'll be alright, Mags. It is just a thank you. Just go and enjoy yourself."

Maggie nodded. "I know. I'm making more of this than I should—"

"But this is the first guy you've gone out with, regardless of the reason, since Scott passed. It's got to be hard for you."

Tears filled Maggie's eyes. "It is, but as long as I keep telling myself that it's not a date, it's a bit easier."

"I think Scott would be fine with this. Besides, Colin's a celebrity; you're a doctor. This is a safe date … oops,

70

not a date, just a dinner. It's one dinner to say 'thank you.' Y'know, nothing more."

Maggie murmured, "I hope so."

The next three days passed by quickly, and on Thursday evening Maggie struggled to find an outfit that she felt comfortable wearing to her dinner with Colin.

How hard can it be to find something to wear? Tossing a pair of black slacks onto a pile of other discarded clothes, she finally decided on a pair of tan slacks and a white cowl neck sweater. *Okay, this'll work. Not too fancy, feels comfortable.*

She let her auburn hair hang loose, pinned up at the sides, which revealed a petite pair of antique gold hoops hanging from her ears. She opened her jewelry box and took out her wedding band, which she rarely wore when working at the hospital. She hesitated for a moment before placing it on her finger.

It's not a date.

She checked her reflection in her dresser mirror and studied her image for a moment. "Don't be ridiculous, Maggie. You can do this." She picked up her keys and headed for her car.

Colin had told her that he would be happy to pick her up, but Maggie had insisted that she drive herself. Her silver Lexus, like her wedding ring, was her source of security. She wanted to be sure she had a way to leave when she wanted to do so. She programmed the GPS for the twenty minute drive to Malibu, then popped in one of Colin's CDs. Valerie had loaned her two of his CDs; one was an older recording of his greatest hits, and the second was a later release of traditional hymns. Maggie was listening to the earlier CD, hoping the various selections would tell her more about the character of the man with whom she was about to spend an evening. She thoroughly lost herself in the music, and almost missed the turn to Colin's home had it not been for the overriding GPS voice reminding her to turn at the next corner.

Maggie pulled up in front of a sprawling, Spanish-style house landscaped with an abundance of shrubs and flowering plants. Exhaling a deep breath, she got out of her car, walked up to the front door, and knocked. Colin opened it immediately.

"I am so glad you came! Please come in." He gestured toward the opulent open living area with three walls of windows providing a panoramic view of the Pacific Ocean.

"Hi, Doc!" greeted Gary. He was walking past the entry carrying a plate piled high with hot wings and French fries. "You two kids have fun." He headed for the staircase.

Before Maggie said a word, he took the stairs two at a time and disappeared. She turned her attention to the living room.

"Wow, this is beautiful!" She stood for a moment gazing out toward the sea. The sun was poised low in the sky; its rays shimmering over the ocean surface.

"Sit wherever you'd like. Would you care for something to drink? I don't have anything alcoholic, but I have every soda imaginable, and juices, plus coffee, and water, of course."

"Coffee would be good." Maggie sauntered over to a window. "What an amazing view!" She watched the waves crashing along the shore about two hundred feet from the patio deck.

Colin returned with the coffee and a soda. "Yeah, that's one of the reasons I rented this one. I like to sit out on the deck in the morning and listen to the waves or take a jog along the beach. We'll see a spectacular sunset in a little while. I suppose I like it here so much because it's so different from where I grew up."

"And where was that?" asked Maggie as she sipped her coffee, noting a hint of cinnamon.

"Scarborough, England. Its beaches aren't nearly as magnificent as these along the Pacific. I really like it here. Maybe I'll move here someday, but for now, renting works nicely for me."

"How long are you here for?"

"Until the album is finished, but … that may change."

"I suppose you travel quite a bit, with the concerts and all?"

"More than I'd like at times."

"It must be exciting doing all that traveling."

The two headed toward the sofa and settled in. Colin leaned back and sipped his soda. "Sometimes, but at other times it can get pretty lonely. Los Angeles is great because I have some friends here, but when we're on the road, it's just one town after the next. England is by far my favorite place to be. Family and friends are there."

Maggie sipped her coffee while taking a good look at the man sitting close to her. Dressed in a long-sleeved maroon shirt and a pair of gray slacks, Colin looked young enough to still be in college, but she had read his biography on the inner jacket of one of his CDs and knew that he was in his late twenties.

He reminds me of Scott. Kind, polite, loves God, and yes, he is incredibly good looking. She fingered her wedding ring.

"So, tell me a little bit about yourself, Maggie. Is it all right if I call you that? After all, I can't call you 'doctor' because that would make this an illegal date." He cocked his head slightly and winked at her.

"It would at that, wouldn't it?" She smiled, relaxing more than she thought she would. "Maggie is fine. Not a lot to tell that you don't already know. I've always wanted to be a doctor. My intention was to be a thoracic surgeon, but I fell in love with emergency medicine during one of my rotations in med school, so that's been my focus ever since. I've lived in California all my life. My brother is also a doctor. He's an oncologist, and you've met my sister-in-law, Valerie; she was your nurse."

"So, medicine runs in the family, and your, uh, husband is a doctor, too?" He gestured toward her wedding ring. Maggie looked at the golden band and replied, "Yes … I mean no, not anymore. Scott, my husband, died shortly after our wedding."

"Wow, I'm sorry. That must have been hard for you." Colin shifted his position to face her. "I'm really sorry; I didn't mean to stir up unhappy memories."

"No apology necessary. It was a little more than three years ago."

Please, please change the subject.

Colin nodded. He sipped his soda before breaking the awkward silence between them. "So, what do doctors do for fun?"

"Well, not much, I'm afraid, or so I've been accused." Maggie chuckled. "I do like to read, but that's about it. My time isn't always my own." She paused. "I do like to go to Santa Molina, Mexico when I can."

"I don't think I've heard of it."

Maggie set her cup down on a solid oak end table. "That doesn't surprise me. It's a little town in east-central Mexico where Scott's brother has a church and a clinic. I like to go and help out when I can. The people there have a lot of medical needs, and I guess I sort of feel close to Scott when I'm there."

"So, you two worked there as a team?"

"Yes, for a short while. After he died, it was hard, but Ryan, my brother-in-law, convinced me to come back on my own. I'm glad I finally did. The first time was the hardest, but each time gets a little bit easier. And I really do feel closer to Scott. He's buried there." *I can't believe how comfortable I feel talking to Colin.* "He died there during an earthquake. It was the hardest thing I've ever had to face, but somehow I got through it. Ryan helped a lot.

"There isn't a day that goes by that I don't think about Scott. I am so thankful for the time we had together. He made such a difference in so many people's lives, including mine."

"Sounds like he was quite a guy."

"He was. I'm doing OK now. Ryan helped me a lot through the first six months or so. I don't pretend to know how God works, but Ryan helped me get to a place where I wasn't angry with Him anymore."

Colin nodded. "I'm glad for that. I don't really remember when my Mum and Dad died, but it took me a long time to get back with the Lord. Made a pretty big change in my life."

"So I've heard." Maggie picked up her coffee cup and sipped. "From rock to gospel."

"Yeah. I wanted my music to make a difference. I hope it has, for some anyway." Colin gulped the last of his soda.

"Do you miss the rock and roll music?"

"Not really. I wasn't ever a hard core rock singer. I was kind of easy listening ... soft rock would be pushing it, I think. I never had a teenybopper following. Now, I have more grandmothers in my fan club." He chuckled.

Maggie laughed. "Really? My nurses sure aren't the grandmother type, and they were quite star-struck when you came into the hospital."

"Really? That's reassuring. Maybe I've still got it, whatever *it* is."

Maggie chuckled and finished her coffee, then set her cup down again. "It would appear so."

"I'm really glad you came tonight, Maggie. It's nice to get a chance to get to know you." When Maggie nodded her reply, Colin took her hand into his own. "Thank you."

"My pleasure," replied Maggie, gently removing her hand from his hold. She gazed around the room and clasped her hands in her lap.

A few moments later Colin said, "So, other than reading, what else do you do in your spare time, if you have any, that is?" The setting sun accented the natural blonde highlights in Colin's hair, and Maggie once again noticed what a strikingly handsome man he was.

"Well, not much actually," stated Maggie, almost apologetically. "I stay pretty busy at work, and even if I'm home, I'm usually on call, so that limits some of what I do. Not a very exciting life, I'm afraid."

"I'd say your life is pretty exciting."

Maggie shifted to face Colin. "Actually, the ER isn't like the emergency rooms you see on television. If they were like that all the time, we'd all burn out in a week. Don't get me wrong, there are very intense moments, but certainly not like it's depicted in the film industry."

"I suppose the media misrepresents a lot of things."

Maggie didn't miss the sadness in his reply. "I take it you've been on the misrepresented side?"

He clasped his hands together and nodded. "Once or twice. It can be a rather painful experience. Not so much for me, but more for my family or friends. That's the very unglamorous side of my work."

"Hmm, well, what do *you* do during your off time?"

"Sleep." He grinned.

"And that's exciting?" teased Maggie. She was thoroughly enjoying their conversation; Colin's laidback manner made it easy for her to relax.

"Strange as it seems, I like to relax with music." He nodded toward the piano. "I find it therapeutic to write. Sometimes it's just instrumental, but sometimes I write lyrics at the same time."

Maggie glanced at the piano. "Would it be out of place for me to ask you to play something now? I really would like to hear you sing."

Colin raised an eyebrow and half-smiled. "Are you sure? Asking a musician to play something is like asking a politician to give a speech. It could go on for hours."

"I don't think I'd mind listening to you for hours, if your live playing is anything like your CDs."

"My goodness, you're a pretty demanding fan," teased Colin as he moved to the grand piano near one side of the living room. He sat down, adjusted the seat, and ran his fingers over the keys playing an arpeggio before he turned to Maggie.

"You're sure?"

"Very."

"OK." Colin began to play a traditional hymn from his most recent album, a simple rendition of *It is Well with My Soul*. Maggie, although unfamiliar with the song, closed her eyes and soaked in the peaceful melody.

This is nice, very nice.

Easily transitioning to other hymns, Colin continued to play for a few more minutes before returning to the loveseat.

Maggie opened her eyes. "You didn't sing."

"I know. I thought I'd save that for another time."

The rest of the evening was filled with small talk, laughter, and comfortable moments of silence between them. Surprising herself, Maggie was saddened to see the evening come to an end.

I wish I didn't have to work tomorrow.

When she stood up to leave, Colin took her hand.

"Maggie, I really had a nice time." He took a slow breath. "I was wondering if I could call you. I'd really like to see you again."

No, no, no! I can't date you!

"I don't know, Colin … most of the time my schedule doesn't allow me— "

"I'm very flexible." Colin gently squeezed her hand. "It could even be a last minute thing, and it wouldn't have to be anything fancy. I mean, you could come here again, or we could go to McDonald's, or I could fly you to Paris. Really, it would be up to you."

Despite trying to stifle it, a chuckle escaped Maggie's lips. "McDonald's or Paris? Now, that's interesting. How would I choose between them?"

"OK, maybe not Paris, I suppose something local would be more practical. Maybe a burger and fries? I could even make them here. You can drive yourself, and you can even pick the day and time."

I can't say yes!

Her wedding ring felt very heavy. She sighed audibly.

Colin clasped her hand in both of his. "Really, what's the worst thing that could happen? We could end up being good friends? That wouldn't be so bad, would it?"

Maggie stared into the sky blue eyes of the man standing in front of her.

I don't think I should do this again. Well, maybe one more time. It could be fun, but after that, no more. Yep, that's really sticking to your principles, Maggie.

She let out a slow, deep breath. "OK. Will Sunday work for you?"

Colin frowned slightly and shook his head as he apologized. "No, I'm sorry. I guess I'm not as flexible as I thought. I'll be at church for most of the day, unless …" a smile creased his lips … "you'd care to join me? You know, with all those people there, it wouldn't even qualify as a real date. What do you say?"

It has been forever since I've been to church. And he's right about one thing, church isn't a date. It's church. Scott would really be pleased that I went.

Maggie returned his smile. "Sure, I'll go with you. What time?"

Colin faltered for a moment. "Hmmm, if you don't mind that I drive, I can pick you up around nine in the morning. Service starts at nine forty-five, well, Sunday school actually. The main service is at eleven."

"You can drive, and I'll be ready at nine."

He put his hands in his pockets and stared at her for a moment.

She tilted her head. "Yes?"

"I know I'm pushing my luck, but would you like to get some lunch after the service? Maybe we could come back here and I could grill some burgers? Or maybe just go out and get some coffee? Whatever you'd like." He shifted his weight and held his breath.

Maggie admitted to herself that she was having a very nice time, and the thought of spending more time with Colin was very enticing. *It only makes sense to have lunch following the service.* "I wouldn't have thought you believed in luck," she chided with a smile.

He grinned sheepishly and shrugged his shoulders.

Maggie smiled at him once more. "Well, luck or no luck, I would love to have lunch with you after church."

"Great! Grilled burgers, it is then!" His smile warmed her heart.

Maggie glanced at her watch, remembering that she had an early shift. Colin walked her out to her car, and held her door open until she had fastened her seat belt.

"Thank you for a really lovely evening," Maggie said through the open window.

"My pleasure, Maggie. I'll see you Sunday." He watched her drive out of sight and put his hands in his pockets. Casting his eyes upward, he spoke softly, "Thank you, Lord, for such a wonderful evening, and for Maggie wanting to go to church with me." He headed into his house whistling *Great Is Thy Faithfulness*.

CHAPTER EIGHT

MAGGIE INHALED THE fragrance of the seasonal flowers in Valerie's small backyard garden. In full bloom, the colorful blossoms filled the air with a floral perfume. It was early morning, and both women had the weekend off. Valerie had prepared a breakfast tray of scones and mini muffins, which they shared while sipping their coffees.

"I can't believe you actually had dinner with Colin Grant!" Valerie took a bite of a banana muffin; her eyes focused across a small patio table on her sister-in-law. "And now you're going out with him again. That is so awesome, Mags!"

"We're going to church, Val, *not* a date."

Valerie tried to frown, but giggled softly. "Yes, of course, call it what you will, but the point is that he asked you out again."

She's loving every minute of this. Maggie simply shook her head. "You are something, dear sister-in-law."

"What? I just think it's about time you got yourself a social life. You're too young to give up on life."

"I have *not* given up on life." Maggie sipped her coffee.

"Oh, really?" Valerie took another bite of her muffin. "What about Dr. Markham? You know, he's been interested in you since forever. I hear he's asked you out a couple of times in the past few months and you've turned him down."

Maggie scowled. "That's some grapevine we have."

"And that new ER resident?"

"Ben Shepherd? You're crazy! He is *not* interested in me. We are just friends." Maggie felt her cheeks grow warm.

"Yeah, well, he'd probably like to be more, I'm sure," retorted Valerie. "Well, it doesn't really matter anymore because you're dating Colin Grant." She got up to refill their cups of coffee.

"I am not!" Maggie called out as her sister-in-law disappeared into the kitchen. She nibbled on a blueberry muffin and watched a hummingbird hover near a hanging basket of pink and white petunias. For the first time in a long time, Maggie felt completely content.

"So, tell me all about it," said Valerie when she returned.

"Hmm … let's see." A coy grin spilled across Maggie's lips. "I believe we started out with quiet conversation." She stopped to take another sip of coffee, then locked her eyes on Valerie.

"I'm waiting." Valerie drummed her fingers on the table top.

Maggie grinned. "OK, OK. We talked a bit about ourselves. You should have seen his house. It was beautiful! And what an ocean view! Colin prepared a delicious dinner, and afterwards, he played the piano for me."

"Oh my goodness, is that romantic or what? And?"

"And that was it. He asked me to go church with him, and I said yes." Maggie finished her last bite of muffin.

"Really?"

"Yes. What else could there be?"

"Did he … you know?"

"I don't know. What are you talking about?"

Valerie leaned forward. "Kiss you, did he kiss you?"

At that moment, a soft muffled hum emanated from Maggie's black purse hanging off the back of her chair. *That was timely!* She pulled the cell phone out, looked at it, and then tossed it back into her purse.

"Who in the world is *texting* you?" Valerie asked, more indignant than curious.

"Not a text," said Maggie. "It's my calendar, reminding me about an appointment later today."

Nobody texts me anymore, Valerie. Not since … not since I lost Scott.

"Well, anyway," continued Valerie, "I was simply pointing out that several men have been interested in you, and you haven't given any of them a chance. But now you don't need to."

Maggie shrugged. "I guess not, especially since I'm dating a *rock star*, right?" Maggie's eyes sparkled as she smiled at Valerie. They both laughed.

Sunday morning at nine o'clock, the doorbell to Maggie's condominium chimed.

I hope I look all right.

She paused by a full-length mirror for a quick check as she headed for the door. Her auburn hair was pinned up with a few tendrils hanging freely. She smoothed her ivory linen skirt, straightened the lilac blouse she wore beneath the matching jacket, and opened the door.

"Morning, Maggie," said Colin, smiling as his eyes moved the length of her body, then returned to meet her gaze. "You look beautiful. Ready?"

"Thank you, and yes, I'm ready."

Maggie noted the shirt he wore beneath the navy blue suit was a close match to his sky blue eyes.

You're not so bad yourself! No wonder my nurses go gaga over you!

They walked to his car, and after helping her into it, he slid behind the wheel of the black BMW. Starting the engine, he backed out slowly from her driveway and onto the main road.

"The church is about a half hour from here. Would you like a cup of coffee or anything before we get there?" he asked as he accelerated into the flow of traffic.

Maggie shook her head. "No. I'm good. This is a very nice car."

"Yeah, I like it. It's a rental. I figure I'm allowed one indulgence, and this is it. My car back home is quite a bit more conservative. I usually ride my bike."

Maggie raised an eyebrow and asked, "You ride a bicycle around?"

Colin chuckled. "No, love. I ride a motorcycle. Whenever the weather is agreeable, I'm usually on it. Unfortunately, London is known for its bad weather, so I spend a lot of time in a car."

"A motorcycle?"

"Yeah, I've always had one, ever since I was a kid. I'd love to take you on a ride sometime. PCH is a gorgeous drive."

"The Pacific Coast Highway? I don't think so." Maggie scowled and shook her head.

Like that's going to happen. I've patched up too many bikers in the ER. No way I'm ending up on a motorcycle.

"Never say never, love."

Settling back in their seats, they continued to chat as Colin drove down the Pacific Coast Highway toward the city of Santa Monica. Time had passed too quickly for Maggie when Colin pulled into the church parking lot.

Just keep on driving, Colin. I don't want this to end!

Reluctant in spirit only, she slipped out of the car after he opened her door. Together, they walked into the sanctuary.

The church was small; the sanctuary would accommodate no more than two hundred people. Each side wall had three stained glass windows, each one representative of one of the parables of Christ. At the front of the church, a large wooden cross stood tall on the wall above the baptistry, a purple cloth draped over its crossbar. Above the cross were the words "I am the resurrection and the life," and a soft white light illuminated both cross and verse. In front of the pulpit was a large fresh floral arrangement of chrysanthemums, tulips, and roses in the center of a mahogany table. Next to the flowers was a large open Bible, slightly elevated toward the congregational area.

A young man near the front of the church looked up as Colin and Maggie entered. A smile spread across his lips when he saw Colin.

"Good morning!" He quickly crossed the length of the church to greet them. As soon as he reached Colin, he shook his hand. "And who is this charming lady with you?"

"Jesse, this is Maggie Devereaux. Maggie, this is Pastor Jesse McClellan. We grew up together in England. I went into the music industry, and he followed a much nobler calling."

Jessie smiled at them both, his soft brown eyes warm and inviting. "Nice to meet you Miss Devereaux." He extended his hand to her.

Jesse McClellan wore a light gray suit with a slightly lighter shaded shirt. A solid black tie completed the outfit.

He's awfully young to be a pastor.

Maggie smiled and shook his hand. "It's a pleasure to meet you, Pastor."

"Colin, I was hoping you'd be here early so I could ask a favor. I was wondering if you would sing something for us during the worship service? I apologize for not calling you earlier this week. I completely forgot, and I was hoping you wouldn't mind."

"Sure, no problem."

Jesse's eyes lit up. "Great!" He glanced at his watch. "I've got to go get my Bible before Sunday school begins. I'll be right back." He hurried off to his office. Colin motioned to a pew and Maggie moved to sit down. Other people began to filter in as it grew closer to the start of the class. Several people came over to greet them, taking time to compliment Colin on his work. He graciously accepted their comments, but always managed to redirect their praise to the Lord.

"Do you get that everywhere you go?" Maggie whispered to Colin, amazed at the attention that came his way.

"Not everywhere," said Colin quietly, "but more often than not. And definitely not as much as before I switched over to Christian music."

"Wow, how do you handle it?"

"Hopefully, with a grateful heart. I would be in a totally different line of work if nobody liked my music. So, I try to remember that when people want to talk with me, or ask for an autograph. Without them, I wouldn't be where I am."

Their attention turned to Jesse, who walked up the aisle to the front of the church. He stood in front of the pews, greeted everyone, then prayed. "Lord, we thank you for this day and the opportunity to meet in Your house to worship You. Please open our hearts to Your Word and what You have for us this day. In Jesus' name, amen."

His Sunday school lesson was about Ruth and Naomi, and as she listened, Maggie wondered about the young Moabite woman. How had Ruth handled the loss of her husband? Did the precious memories of him remain alive in her heart, as hers did with those of Scott?

During the class, Colin sat close to Maggie, his arm around her on the back of the pew, but his attention was focused on Jesse. His Bible lay open in his lap, and Maggie noticed that he, like Scott, also made notes in the margins. As Jesse closed the Sunday school class with a short prayer, Maggie's thoughts drifted to the times when she had sat beside Scott in his church. She stared down at her wedding ring. *I wish you were here with me.*

With the worship service scheduled to begin at eleven o'clock, the small church began to fill, and as the people moved into the pews, Maggie overheard bits of conversations, many peppered with comments about how God had touched their lives in one way or another during the previous week.

This is so much like Scott's church. Everyone here seems so, so content. Just like Scott was ... just like Colin is. How can they be so—

Her thoughts were interrupted as a young man stood up and welcomed everyone to the service. Maggie sat comfortably next to Colin listening to the announcements, then the same man turned toward the choir. With robust voices, the choir sang their first number, the song telling of a coming day when Christ would return for His church in glory. At its conclusion, the music director led the entire church in the singing of several traditional hymns, before Jesse came to the pulpit and addressed the congregation.

"Good morning. As many of you know, a very dear friend of mine has been in town, and many of you have met him during these past few weeks." Jesse grinned and glanced at

Colin. "I've known Colin Grant longer than I can remember, and the Lord has given him an incredible talent for music, so I've asked him to sing for us today. Colin, please come on up and share a song with us."

Colin walked over to the piano. He sat down and adjusted the microphone.

"It took me a long time to realize that what I needed most in my life was Jesus, but when I did, it was the greatest day of my life. I will never forget that day when Jesus came into my heart and saved me."

A few amens sounded throughout the sanctuary as Colin continued. "No matter how far I had gone, or how much I resisted, Jesus was always there calling for me to come home." Maggie noticed that, although his voice was strong and steady, the emotion behind his words was impossible to miss.

He began to play the piano, and then sang from his heart.

> *Softly and tenderly Jesus is calling, calling for you and for me,*
> *See on the portals, He's waiting and watching, watching for you and for me.*
> *Come home, come home, ye who are weary, come home.*
> *Earnestly, tenderly, Jesus is calling, calling o sinner, come home.*

He sang all the verses in the song, and ended by saying, "It was really good to come home, to Him." There was a quiet hush in the church as Colin returned to his seat.

Jesse returned to the podium. "Thank you, Colin, that was truly a blessing. Isn't it great to know that no matter who you are or what you've done, Jesus is calling you? He wants to have a relationship with you. In fact, He gave His life to have that relationship." Jesse prayed once more, then opened his Bible and began to read from the sixth chapter of 1 Timothy. After reading the entire chapter, he focused on verse twelve. *Fight the good fight of faith, lay hold on eternal life, whereunto thou are also called, and hast professed a good profession before many witnesses.*

"What is faith?" he began. "It is not just one simple act of belief, but a lifestyle. Galatians, chapter 3, verse 11 tells us that 'The just shall live by faith.' Our faith must be more than a Sunday event. It should be an everyday event. Your life should reflect your faith in everything you do, and everything you say.

"The Bible uses several examples to help us understand what faith is. For example, in Acts 14:27, Paul speaks of how God 'opened the door of faith unto the Gentiles.' There is also the household of faith to all believers, as spoken of in Galatians 6:10. We have to walk through that door and dwell in that household if our faith is genuine, but what does that mean?"

Jesse stepped to the side of the podium, leaning his left arm on it. "If you turn in your Bibles to 1 Thessalonians chapter 1, verse 3, you will see that faith is demonstrated through work. The Scriptures repeatedly tell us that our faith is our work, and that faith without works is dead." He moved back behind the podium and read from his opened Bible. "1 Thessalonians 1:3 says, 'Remembering without ceasing your work of faith.' Our works are a reflection of our faith, and those works speak to both believers and nonbelievers. To other Christians, our works should encourage, edify, and strengthen them. To nonbelievers, our works should point the way to Christ."

He spent the next half hour explaining the fight of faith, and how the Christian has victory in overcoming the world through personal faith.

Jesse concluded his message by reminding the congregation that Christ continues to be the foundation of their faith. "Our faith centers on the living Savior, Jesus Christ. The book of Hebrews tells us that 'Without faith, it is impossible to please Him,' but 'with faith, all things are possible to him that believeth.' Where is your faith today? Is there a time in your life when you asked Christ to forgive your sins and become Savior of your life? Faith is believing that Jesus is the way, the truth, and the life, and that no man can come to God the Father without God the Son. If you have never surrendered your life to Christ, let today be the day of your salvation."

Jesse invited anyone to come forward to the altar if they had a spiritual need, including that of salvation. Several individuals walked up to the front of the church and knelt at the altar to pray.

Colin had his hands folded together and rested his arms on the pew in front of him, his head bowed, his eyes closed in prayer. Maggie sat very still, thinking about the words Jesse had spoken. *I believe in Jesus; I know I do, so why is my faith so different from Colin's. It's just like it was with Scott. But, why?* Her discomfort faded quickly as Jesse ended the service with a short prayer. She followed Colin as he led her toward the exit where Jesse stood. She waited patiently as the two men talked briefly.

"It was so nice meeting you, Maggie. I hope to see you again," said Jesse, his smile genuine.

"Thank you, Pastor. I enjoyed the service." Walking to the car alongside Colin, she pondered the message and its relevance to her.

"How'd you like the service?" asked Colin as they walked into his house. He tossed his jacket on the back of the sofa and rolled up his shirt sleeves.

"It was nice," replied Maggie. She followed his lead and hung her ivory jacket on the back of a dining room chair. "Especially the special music."

Colin grinned. "You're the kind of fan I like." He walked through the open archway into his kitchen. "Soda, lemonade, or water?" he called out. "I don't have the coffee on, but I could start a pot if you like."

"Soda would be nice. Diet, if you have it. Do you need some help?" said Maggie as she trailed after Colin into the kitchen.

"Sure. Would you mind slicing that?" He pointed to a cutting board where he had already placed a plump red tomato and a small paring knife. He set a head of lettuce on the counter next to Maggie, and then got their drinks.

"Plates?" Maggie was poised to open any cabinet.

"Above you to the right." He removed a serving plate with four hamburger patties on it from the refrigerator. "Cheese?"

Maggie turned to look at Colin and smiled coyly. "No, I think that's hamburger."

"A doctor and a comedian? You are very talented. Cheese on your burger?"

"Oh, that's what you meant. Cheese would be nice, thank you," she answered, softly laughing as she sliced the tomatoes. She placed them on a dinner plate, and then peeled off a few leaves of lettuce, washed and dried them, and put them next to the tomatoes. While Colin went out on the patio to start the grill, Maggie glanced around at the immaculate kitchen.

"You must have a maid," she remarked when Colin came back in.

"Not me. I'm the youngest of three. I had the job of cleaning the house each week. I suppose it was good training because now I keep things fairly tidy. Well, most of the time. Just don't go upstairs and look in the bedroom. It's pretty much a disaster right now.

"When I knew you were coming, I made sure the kitchen, living room, and lower bath were clean, hoping to impress you. The top floor, well, that's not exactly worthy of the Good Housekeeping seal." Colin grinned as he set a bowl of potato salad and one of coleslaw on the chocolate brown granite counter.

"I'm impressed."

"Well, good. It worked then. Any preference?" He indicated the two salads.

"Um ... no, either one is fine."

He pulled out a package of buns from the pantry. "Toasted or steamed?"

"Toasted?" she tilted her head. "It really doesn't matter."

"Boy, for someone who has to make lifesaving decisions all day, these simple ones seem to throw you," Colin nudged her with an elbow as she stood beside him. "Toasted. A very good choice, Doc. Be right back."

Maggie watched Colin head out to the patio again. *I am really having a nice time. I know I said I wouldn't have a third date with him, but we are just friends. I mean, really, the worst thing that would happen would be us becoming really good friends. There's certainly nothing wrong with that. Besides, he may not even ask me for another—*

"Just about ready!"

Maggie came back to the moment and carried the rest of their lunch out on a serving tray to the patio. "Sorry, I was daydreaming."

He took the tray from Maggie and helped her set the table. "Really? I didn't know doctors did that. They always seem so serious."

"Hey, I have a fun side!"

"Sure you do, Doc, sure you do."

Maggie feigned indignation and put her hands on her hips. "Careful, buddy, or you'll be wearing ketchup!"

Colin held his hands up as if surrendering. "Point taken. I'll back off, ma'am!" He winked at her. "I hope you're not too upset to eat because these burgers are ready!"

She giggled and carried their plates over to him.

"I'll get over it. These smell delicious!"

After lunch, they spent the remainder of the afternoon talking and relaxing on the patio. As the sun neared the horizon, Maggie reflected on the day, and was very glad she had decided to spend it with Colin.

"This has been so nice, Colin. I'm so glad you invited me to church … and lunch."

"I'm glad you accepted, Maggie." Colin looked at his watch. "Wow! Time sure gets away quickly. I need to get back for the evening service." He stood up, then looked at her.

He's waiting for me to say something. Should I go with him? What if … no, I am not going to go down that path. We are just good friends who enjoy each other's company.

She smiled at him and held out her hand. "Let's go!"

"It's a shame today has to end," commented Colin as he exited from the drive-through lane of a Chick-fil-A restaurant. "It's been a great day." He handed Maggie a bag that contained their impromptu dinner.

"I could do this again." She pulled out a waffle fry and popped it into her mouth.

"Really?" Colin glanced at Maggie, and then returned his gaze to the road. "You'd do it again?"

Oops, I opened the door on that one. What do I say now?

Maggie knew that her response would be pivotal for the future of their relationship, but she also knew that she had really enjoyed being with Colin. Convinced she could keep the relationship at a friendship level, she committed herself to that.

"Yes, I would." She glanced sideways at Colin. "I thought today was wonderful. There wasn't one part of it that I didn't like."

"Hmm, I thought it was going to be a lot harder than this to get you to see me again."

"I guess it's that smooth singing style of yours coupled with your British charm," teased Maggie as she sipped her diet soda.

Colin laughed. "British charm? Is that what it is?"

"Something like that."

CHAPTER NINE

SITTING IN THE cafeteria, Maggie glanced at her watch: 8:30 A.M. Thirty minutes until she ended her shift. Valerie sat down across the table from Maggie with a tray laden with two ham and egg croissants, two granola bars, and two cups of coffee. It had been almost six hours since Maggie had taken a break.

Maggie removed the lid from her coffee and took a sip.

"Sounds like it's been pretty hectic," said Valerie as she took a bite of her breakfast sandwich.

Maggie opened her sandwich, sprinkled some pepper on it, and took a bite. "That's an understatement," she said, rubbing the back of her neck. "You're walking into one chaotic department this morning. It's been a horrible night. Ben and I have been running ourselves ragged."

"I'm sorry. Sometimes I wish I worked for a dermatologist. I mean, really, how many skin emergencies could there be?" She tore off a small section of the croissant and popped it into her mouth.

"Hmm, acute acne attack?" They both giggled.

At that moment, both their pagers went off. Simultaneously, they pulled them out of their pockets and groaned. "Dermatology is starting to look better by the moment! So much for a quiet end to my shift." Maggie stuffed her pager back in her pocket.

Valerie stuck a granola bar in her pants pocket, and took a few swallows of her coffee.

They rose, put their breakfast items in the collection area, and marched back to the emergency room.

Valerie frowned as she entered the nurses' station. "What've we got?"

"Bus accident," the clerk informed them. "They're expecting quite a few victims."

Valerie gave her sister-in-law a hug. "Thanks for the breakfast, what little of it we got to eat. Guess you'll be here a little longer, huh, Dr. D? See you around!"

Valerie disappeared into the supply closet, and Maggie headed off to assess the status of each treatment room. She wanted to be as ready as possible for anything that might come in from the accident. "Expect the unexpected," she murmured to herself as she nodded to two other ER doctors emerging from the elevators.

The emergency room was functioning under a quiet veil of controlled chaos when Maggie reemerged from the treatment area. Amidst the usual coughs and crying from those who, for whatever reason, preferred an ER visit to a scheduled doctor's appointment, was the cacophony of paramedic and nurse commentaries, the clamor of medical equipment as it was moved from one treatment area to the next, and the irritated voices of those who were still waiting to be seen.

Rising above the din was the voice of Valerie Garrett. A commanding presence in the midst of the waiting area, she began barking orders to the staff. Immediately, triage and treatment began to assume some semblance of order. Maggie swiftly entered the nurses' station, scanned the triage board for current patients, and mentally noted their status.

"Dr. Devereaux, we need you in treatment room four!" called a nurse from behind her. Maggie headed straight for the room. As she entered, a nurse began to recite pertinent information to Maggie, who then acted upon the data received. This scene repeated itself over and over throughout the morning, and it would be early afternoon before either Maggie or Valerie would have an opportunity to sit down and take a much-needed break.

Ambulance after ambulance arrived with the injured. Maggie took a deep breath, and scanned the triage board once more. Each time a name was erased, another one took its place.

When is this going to end?

She had already sent four patients straight to surgery, and two others were airlifted to the regional hospital that specialized in spinal cord trauma. One woman gave birth to a healthy baby boy in one of the ER corridors, completely unrelated to the bus accident, which lifted the spirits of the working staff. Most of the injuries were not critical, but severe enough to warrant a stay overnight for observation or additional treatment. After the initial triage, Maggie spent much of her time suturing lacerations or debriding wounds.

As she exited the treatment area, the ambulance bay doors opened, and paramedics hurriedly guided a gurney into the triage area. Maggie quickly fell into step with them.

"This is the driver. He's in pretty bad shape. It took a while to extricate him," explained the paramedic. He rapidly reported the current vital signs and the treatment initiated in the field.

Maggie did an immediate assessment, and quickly found herself engaged in a losing battle for the elderly man's life.

"Get me two units of O-neg blood, stat!" she called out to no one in particular. One of the nurses rushed to the phone and called the lab, then returned to her post by the bedside.

"Can I help?"

Maggie glanced up and saw Ben Shepherd move to the opposite side of the bed.

"I need an airway," Maggie stated urgently. *If we can't get an airway in fast, he'll never make it.* She knew that each minute without oxygen could lead to permanent brain damage, and the bus driver was struggling to breathe.

"I'm on it," said Shepherd.

Maggie looked up at the cardiac monitor, then at a nurse. "If you can't get that in, we're going to need a central line," she stated as a nurse tried in vain to reestablish a blown peripheral intravenous line.

Valerie moved quickly to assist in inserting the new IV line. It only took a few seconds before she found another vein, inserted a new needle, and felt it pop as it penetrated the vessel wall. She carefully threaded the flexible catheter into the vein after getting a small flashback of blood into the needle.

"It's in, Doctor."

Maggie placed her stethoscope to the chest of the bus driver and listened for a definitive heartbeat. She only heard the breath sounds of the air artificially pumped in by the respiratory technician. She shook her head in frustration at the same time that Valerie confirmed what she had feared.

"He's in v-fib!"

Maggie glanced up at the cardiac monitor once again, noting the erratic heartbeat. She took the defibrillator electrode paddles from Valerie.

"Charging to 250."

"Clear!"

Everyone stepped away from the bed as Maggie discharged the paddles simultaneously, delivering an electrical shock to the man's heart. The bus driver's body arched slightly, and then collapsed back onto the bed.

"Still in v-fib ... charging to 300!"

"Clear!"

Another electrical charge jolted through the man's body.

"Get me bicarb on board," Maggie ordered, knowing the intravenous administration of sodium bicarbonate would counter the acidic response of the quivering heart. She repeated the defibrillation sequence once more, before the bus driver's heart reluctantly returned to a somewhat irregular, but acceptable, rhythm. The medical team worked fervently, but the worn heart refused to maintain its pace, and the pulsations both slowed and weakened.

"His pressure's dropping! Can't get a pulse—"

"Starting compressions."

"Epinephrine," commanded Maggie to a nurse on her left, hoping the drug would stimulate the patient's circulatory system.

"On board," came the reply.

"C'mon, c'mon," coaxed Maggie as she looked at the cardiac monitor. *Don't you die on me!*

The medical team valiantly continued their attempts to resuscitate their patient, but after twenty minutes, Maggie reluctantly made the decision to terminate their efforts. She looked up at the clock. "Time of death, fourteen oh-one." The room became strangely quiet, as it always did when someone was pronounced dead. Everyone worked automatically, preparing the body for its final trip to the morgue.

"Is the family here?" Maggie asked anyone who was listening.

"Not yet."

"Would you like me to talk to them, Maggie?" asked Shepherd.

"Thanks, but no. I'll speak with them." Although Maggie had witnessed death many times, it always had a sobering effect upon her. It grieved her to think that someone now had to go through the pain of losing a loved one, just as she had done when Scott died.

"Let me know when they're here, OK Val?" Maggie pulled off her gloves and flung them into a waste basket. She walked directly to the staff lounge, upset by the loss of her patient. *I did everything right; I know I did. I can't believe I lost him.*

She sat down in a chair and slammed her fists on the armrests. She mentally reviewed the events of the bus driver's code, and affirmed that she wouldn't have done anything differently. Still, she felt frustrated that she couldn't save the man's life. A few minutes later, one of the staff nurses informed her that the bus driver's wife and children had arrived.

Maggie gently broke the news of the death to his family, and remained in the waiting room holding the weeping wife in her arms. In between sobs, the older woman thanked Maggie for all she had done, and Maggie felt an agonizing sorrow for her. Returning to the lounge, Maggie took a deep breath, allowing her thoughts to drift to Scott, his warm smile, and the emptiness she felt whenever her mind wandered to that fateful day in Santa Molina.

Why did you have to leave me? I need you, and I miss you so much.

Gradually, as she rested her head on the back of the sofa, her mental image of Scott faded and was replaced with that of Colin Grant. Impulsively, she pulled her phone out of her pocket and stared at it. She took a deep breath and punched in his private number. His phone rang once, twice, and just as she was going to end the call, she heard his voice.

"Maggie? Is everything OK?"

"Yes, it's just been a long, hard day, and I ... I hoped you weren't busy. I—"

I can't believe I called him. What was I thinking?

She fumbled for the right words. "I thought it would be nice to talk to you. I mean, I thought ... I'm sorry. You're probably busy. I shouldn't have—"

"No apology needed. I was just working on a song. Are you really all right?"

"Yes. I just ... well, I honestly don't know why I called."

"Are you off work?"

"Yes. Things have finally settled down, and I'm just about to head home. I just had a moment in the lounge, and I was thinking about you, and I, well, I just wanted—"

"No explanation needed," said Colin. "I'm glad you did. Want some company? I could swing by and pick you up. We could grab a bite to eat, watch the sunset, and I promise I'll have you back home before you know it. Maybe it would help you relax."

Maggie's hand trembled. "I don't want to impose."

"It's not an imposition, Maggie, really. I can be there in no time at all."

Maggie hesitated.

She heard him ask, "Is it better if I pick you up at your place or the hospital?"

Before she could stop herself, she replied, "My house would be best, I think. Give me about thirty minutes." She hung up and took another deep breath. She walked over to her locker, leaned against it with her head down on her arm, not hearing the door open and close behind her.

"Mags? You OK?"

Maggie turned to face Valerie, and managed a small, tired smile. "Yes, Val. I'm fine. I think I'm just tired. I'm going to head on home. Thanks for all you did in there."

"No problem. We make a good team, you and I. But I don't need these kinds of days." Valerie stared at the ground, then looked up at Maggie. "You want to go over and crash at our place? We're closer."

Should I tell her? No, not now. I don't think I could handle the inquisition.

"No, thank you though. I think I'll just head on home."

Valerie gave her a hug. "Then I'll see you tomorrow." She paused, then said, "You did good today, Mags. Real good. Especially with the driver's wife. You're the best." Valerie squeezed Maggie's hands, then left the room.

After hanging her lab coat in her locker, Maggie took one more walk through the ER to make sure things had settled down, then left the hospital.

Turning the key to her door, she opened it and hurried upstairs to shower and change into a t-shirt emblazoned with *Stanford University* on the front of it, a pair of stone-washed jeans, and a pair of barely used tennis shoes. Just as she finished securing her hair into a ponytail, the doorbell rang. Bounding down the stairs, she paused briefly, brushed her bangs from her forehead, then opened the door.

Colin stood there in a pair of khaki pants and a white polo shirt. His smile was radiant as he produced a small bouquet of flowers between him and Maggie. "I thought these might brighten up the rest of your day."

"Oh, Colin, *thank you.*" She breathed in the floral fragrance. "Let me put them in a vase, and I'll be right back. Please, come in." She disappeared into the kitchen.

Colin took advantage of the moment to look around Maggie's home. It was decorated in pale blues and greens, and several paintings of outdoor scenes hung on the walls. He walked over to the fireplace mantel, noting the matching candles at each end and some photos of various people between them. *Hmm ... well, this one is Valerie. I guess this is Maggie's brother. Who's this guy with Maggie? I'll bet it's her husband. She sure looks happy.*

He noticed several potted plants placed throughout the room, which, combined with the soft lighting, created a relaxing environment. He sat on the sofa, picked up a small photo album from the coffee table, and began to thumb through it. It contained pictures of children, mostly Hispanic. A few of the pictures had the same unknown man in them, except now and then he had a stethoscope around his neck.

Yes, this has to be Scott. Wonder where this is? Wow, these children need some serious medical care!

"Those are my kids." Maggie's voice interrupted his perusal of the album.

"Your kids?" Colin queried, looking up at her.

"Well, that's what I call them. Those are some of the kids I've worked with during my trips to Mexico. Last year, a plastic surgeon friend of mine went with me, and he arranged to have three of our kids' physical deformities repaired at no charge here in the States. I also took a ton of vaccinations and inoculated as many children as possible against diseases we've almost eradicated here, so I think of them as my kids."

"This is Santa Molina?" He thumbed through a few more pictures. He looked up and saw Maggie nod her head. "I can totally see you doing this." Colin replaced the book on the table and stood up. "There is so much about you I'd love to get to know."

"You'll have to come with me sometime," she said as she put on a light gray jacket.

Her casual invitation caught Colin off guard, but he tucked the thought into the back of his mind.

"Ready?" When she nodded, he escorted her to the passenger side of his car. After she was seated, he moved to the driver's side and slid in.

"I love this car! It is so comfortable."

"Good, then you should be able to relax without any problem," said Colin as he maneuvered onto the highway. "Where would you like me to pick up dinner?"

"Anywhere is fine." She tilted the back of her seat down a bit and closed her eyes, then quickly reopened them. "Do you mind?"

"Not at all, love." *Thank you, Lord, for Maggie calling me when she needed someone.* He glanced over at her, saw that her eyes were closed once more, and began to quietly hum.

Although the drive to his house was not long, Maggie had almost fallen asleep when Colin brought the car to a stop in the cobblestone driveway. She opened her eyes slowly, and looked outside.

"I didn't know singers listened to their own music," she said as she stretched.

Colin turned toward Maggie and chuckled. "I was not listening to my own CD."

"But I heard your songs."

"That was me. I like to sing while I drive. I tried to keep it low. Hope I didn't keep you awake."

"Oh, no you didn't. In fact it was very nice. I just assumed you put on a CD."

"No, I didn't, but I'm glad you liked the singing." He helped Maggie out of the car. "Let's go out on the deck and eat. It's going to be a gorgeous sunset."

Maggie followed him through the sliding door and stretched out on a lounge chair. She took the glass of soda he brought her and sipped it slowly.

"Hmm, this is nice."

Colin sat on a matching chair beside her. The rhythmic sound of the waves washed over both of them. "I love to sit out here and just listen to the ocean. It always helps me relax. I hope it'll do the same for you."

"It already has." Maggie pulled her legs up to her chest.

"Do doctors talk about their day, or do they just keep it all inside?" He handed her a napkin and a chicken avocado wrap he pulled from a sack. He removed another for himself and began to unwrap it as Maggie took a bite out of hers.

"Well, it all depends. As long as the patient-doctor confidentiality thing remains intact, we can talk about it, but I usually don't share my day with anyone except maybe my brother or his wife. Sometimes it can seem rather gory or depressing."

Colin listened while munching on his wrap. *Don't push her, Colin. Just give her some space.* He drank some of his soda, and waited as he watched the sunlight ripple across the ocean surface. Several gulls circled overhead. Maggie remained silent about the activities of the day. She seemed to be deep in thought, and he did not want to intrude.

"Colin?"

"Yes?"

"I'd love to hear you sing some more."

"Now?"

"Yes. Would you?"

"Sure, if you'd like. Stay here. I'll be right back." He returned with a beautiful acoustic Fender guitar. Sitting at the bottom of the lounge chair she was resting on, he began to softly tune the strings.

"You sang so nice in the car, I thought it'd be wonderful to hear you when I'm more awake."

"No problem. Singers always like an audience. My brothers used to have to listen to all my new songs when I first started writing. I had to beg them to listen. They'd usually roll their eyes and protest, but in the end, they'd listen and critique, which was what I needed, but not always what I wanted. Usually, I'd take their suggestions and see if I could refine the song, then come back for more punishment." His eyes reflected the admiration in his voice. "They gave me a lot of encouragement in my career."

"Sounds like they're pretty special."

"Yeah. They pretty much raised me after Mum and Dad died. Made sure I had everything. I don't suppose I'll ever know how much they sacrificed for me, but I know that if it weren't for them, and the Lord, I wouldn't be where I am today."

He began to gently pluck the strings creating a soothing melody. His fingers moved effortlessly over the instrument, then he began to sing.

> I am weak, but Thou art strong, Jesus keep me from all wrong,
> I'll be satisfied as long, as I walk, let me walk close to Thee.
> Just a closer walk with Thee, grant it Jesus, is my plea,
> Daily walking close to Thee, let it be, dear Lord, let it be.

After finishing the verses, he continued to strum the strings, creating a beautiful composition to accompany the rhythmic sounds of the Pacific Ocean.

"You play beautifully."

"Thank you." He set the guitar down on the lounge chair and extended his hand toward her. "Could I interest you in a walk on the beach?"

She took his hand and stood up. "If I can't sit here forever and listen to you sing, the walk will have to do."

Colin led her down to the sand. They walked for a while without speaking, simply enjoying the company of one another.

Maggie broke the silence. "Do you get to L.A. often?"

"Only if I have a tour that brings me here, which isn't too often anymore, or if I'm doing some recording. I try and combine the two, so I don't have to make too many separate trips here." He paused and glanced over at her. "But I may be here more often from now on." His comment faded into the crashing waves. *She's still holding my hand.*

They continued down the shoreline without speaking; the only sounds were the breaking waves and the intermittent cries of the gulls.

Hearing Maggie sigh, Colin broke the silence. "Bad day?"

"Sort of ..." She slowly unfolded the day's events, and when she finished, Colin stopped and turned her toward him. He noticed a few tears had run down her cheeks. He gently wiped them away, and then cupped her face in his hands. Their eyes met, and, for a moment, all Colin wanted to do was to take Maggie in his arms and kiss away all her pain and sadness. The struggle to resist the temptation before him was overwhelming.

Help me, Lord. I know that I should not get romantically involved with someone who isn't a Christian, but it's so hard. All I want to do is hold her and protect her from the pain. Give me the strength I need to do what I know is right.

He willed himself to only brush her hair from her eyes, and then forced his hands into his pockets.

Taking a deep breath, he softly said, "You are an amazing lady, Maggie. I cannot begin to imagine what you must go through every day. What an amazing gift you have."

Maggie looked up at Colin, puzzled. "Gift?"

"Yes, the gift of healing. God uses you to bring health and well-being to countless people. You don't know who is coming through those doors each day. You've been trained, I assume, in almost every aspect of medicine, and when those people come in, you have to take a good, hard look at whatever they present, make some kind of diagnosis, then treat them. Sometimes, the ones who look to you for healing won't be able to find it, so you have to be the one to help them, or their families, come to terms with death." He stared out over the horizon. "Not just anyone can do that, Maggie. Not the way you do. I know firsthand how you act in the ER, and it's pretty remarkable."

They resumed their walk as Colin continued.

"When I was in the hospital, I'll admit that I was scared. I didn't really want to tell anyone that because ... oh, I don't know, maybe I was trying to be strong. Anyway, I think inwardly, I was glad that Gary insisted I get checked out because I was thinking 'What if it is my heart?' I knew that heart attacks weren't age specific, so I had this fear that maybe I had had one."

"You didn't seem afraid, if that helps any."

"Well, I was ... in fact, I was also struggling greatly to put everything in God's hands. That's never easy to do. But I know He's in control of everything—"

"You really believe that?"

"Yeah, I do. I don't understand it all, or how He works, but I do believe He is completely in total control. In fact, I believe our meeting and becoming friends was also divinely orchestrated."

"You really think God cares about who we meet?"

Colin looked over at Maggie and smiled. "I think He cares about everything that happens to us, good and bad."

Maggie stared at the sand. "Then why does He let bad things happen to us?"

Please, Lord, help me say the right thing, so she'll understand.

Colin thought for a moment. "I don't have all the answers, Maggie. I guess that's where the faith aspect comes into play. The Bible tells us a lot about God's character, but it doesn't give us all the answers in life. You see, my pericarditis was not a good thing, but a very good thing came from it—my meeting you. When bad things happen, God can use it for something good."

"You really think so?"

"That I know without a doubt. The Bible says that 'All things work together for good to them that love God, to them who are the called according to his purpose.' So, no matter what happens to me, I know that God will somehow use it for good. Unfortunately, that doesn't always remove my fears. I still struggle with that, but I also know He's working on that, too."

"You remind me of Scott."

Colin smiled. "I'll take that as a compliment."

"It is. Scott's faith was strong, like yours. I'm sure you can probably tell that I don't have that same quality. I do believe in God, but there's something about the two of you, and your faith, that I just don't understand. I guess sometimes it's hard to reconcile a loving God with all the pain and suffering … and death that I see in the ER."

Colin nodded. "I can only imagine what that must be like for you; how did Scott handle that?"

Maggie shook her head. "I don't know. We never talked about that. I never asked, and he never offered. I guess we both thought we had plenty of time to get to those kinds of questions. I was going to talk to Ryan, my brother-in-law, about it, the day … Scott died, but we never had the chance after that. I suppose I didn't want to make the opportunity any more. I really wasn't in the frame of mind to talk about religion at that time."

"I can understand that." Colin glanced at the sun heading towards the horizon, but Maggie seemed lost in their conversation.

"I don't get how you can be so, so personal with God. I mean, you talk about Him as if He were right here … walking with you like … like a good friend."

"I guess that's because I believe He *is* right here."

Maggie stopped and turned to him. "Like right here? Right now? Walking with us?"

When he nodded, she continued. "That just doesn't make any sense to me. We're just two people in a world of billions. Why would God care enough about us to be right here? There has to be more important things for Him to do."

Man, she's asking tough questions, Lord. I don't want to blow it. Please help me out here. "Maggie, I'm not a Bible scholar, but I'm going to try my best to explain what I believe to be true about God."

She nodded and walked quietly beside Colin, staring at the sand as he spoke, still holding his hand.

Colin took a deep breath and turned them back in the direction they had come. "I know God cares about me, and you, because the Bible says so. I believe the Bible is the complete, inspired Word of God, and it's the foundation of my faith—Scott's too, I presume. Anyway, everything I'm going to tell you comes from that viewpoint. That's where my faith begins. Without my belief in the Scriptures, my faith would have nothing to stand on.

"I've been a pretty good guy in my life. Despite the circumstances that could have hindered my life's course, I think I turned out pretty decent, but I was really missing something … inside here." He tapped his chest over his heart.

"I was very successful in my career. I had grown up believing in God, but I didn't really have any relationship with Him, so to speak. God was distant. Well, actually, I was distant from Him. He was Someone I thought about on Christmas and Easter, but other than that I pretty much ignored Him. I was mostly into myself. One day, I realized that something was missing from my life. I had money, fame, good friends, but I didn't have the answer to my discontent. So, I decided to do some soul searching. I took some time off from my career, returned home to my family, and revisited my old church."

Maggie glanced at the setting sun, its rays washing the sky with gold and orange and red. "Why? What made you decide to go there?"

"I suppose most people would say it was just chance, but I believe somehow the Holy Spirit of God led me there. I had decided to go for a drive, and when I passed the church that Mum and Dad used to go to, I felt compelled to go in. I can't really explain it, but I know it was not chance." When she didn't speak, he continued.

"I walked around the grounds and ended up in the cemetery where Mum and Dad were buried. I found their graves and stood wondering what I was doing there. It was then the pastor saw me and came out. I introduced myself and we started talking. When he invited me to the next Sunday's service, I decided to go.

Colin took a deep breath of the invigorating salt air. "That first Sunday was amazing. The people were so genuinely nice. There were a few who knew who I was … mainly the young adults, but to most I was simply an anonymous visitor. Everyone was just as welcoming as could be. It kind of blew me away to have people ask me who I was and where I was from. When I told a few of the older members my name, they would call out to someone else and say, 'Hey, this is Peter and Elisabeth's son, Colin!' I wasn't the famous singer to these folks; I was Peter and Elisabeth's kid. That was something." Colin smiled as he reflected upon his first encounter with the members of his parents' church.

"Sorry, I'm digressing here. Let me get back to what you asked."

"No, it's fine. I am really interested in your story." She squeezed his hand.

"That day felt so good, Maggie. And even though I didn't really know a soul there, it felt like I had come home."

"Sounds like that could be a song," she commented as she kicked up some sand in front of them.

"Yes, I suppose it could be. Well, anyway, I had some more visits with the pastor, continued coming to church, and I realized I was missing the personal aspect of salvation—the real relationship that comes after getting saved. I mean, I had asked Christ to be my Savior as a kid, but I never made a commitment to serve Him, until that day. It was then that I totally surrendered my life to Him." He paused and glanced at the sun resting on the horizon. "Now, back to your questions."

"Wait. What do mean you 'surrendered your life'?"

"It means I made a conscious decision to live my life in a way that would honor Christ. You see, Maggie, Jesus bought me with His blood when He died on the cross, so I belong to Him. Whatever He wants me to do in my life, I've made a conscious decision to do it. It's not easy by any means. I still struggle with my own will every day, and I'm often on my knees asking for His forgiveness for putting my will above His, but I'm trying."

Maggie frowned. "So, believing in Him isn't enough?"

"Not really. The Bible says even the demons believe in Christ. It's the act of accepting that's the key. See, we're all sinners and the only way to be forgiven is through Christ. It's a matter of accepting God at His Word, believing that Jesus' death on the cross is the only way to have reconciliation with God, and then asking Christ to do what He said He died for ... to forgive you and become the Lord and Savior of your life."

"So that's why you switched to gospel music?"

"Yes. I want to serve Him with my life, and the only thing I really know how to do is sing, so the switch to gospel made sense to me. Now that He's given me a measure of success, I'm hoping I can do more for Him, but He hasn't really shown me the direction to go yet."

Maggie remained silent as she walked beside Colin. Her heart was pounding; she had so many questions she wanted to ask, but she didn't know where to begin.

With the sun disappearing, Maggie pulled her jacket closer around her and turned toward the ocean, and Colin moved behind her, his hands securely in his pants pockets.

"Maggie, you asked if God cares about us. The answer is yes. He's always with us. He loves us more than we can imagine, and He would never abandon any of us."

"You think God cares about me even if I don't feel the same way about Him that you do?"

"Always. His love for you isn't contingent upon your love for Him. Do you actually think God's brought you this far just to let you go?"

She turned around and looked directly into Colin's blue eyes. "What do you mean 'brought me this far'?"

"God is definitely interested in your life, Maggie. You may not be searching for Him, but He definitely is waiting for you."

CHAPTER TEN

DO YOU REALLY know what you're getting yourself into?" asked the tall doctor sitting across from Maggie. His thick black hair framed his rectangular face and furrowed brow. The hospital cafeteria was almost empty after the lunch hour rush.

"What exactly do you mean, Will? I am not *getting* into anything," protested Maggie. She took a bite of the ham and cheese sandwich she had just purchased.

Will sat back in his chair. "Val told me all about this guy you're seeing. To begin with, don't you think he's a bit young for you? Secondly, he's a rock star, for goodness sake. Are you insane?"

"I had no idea you'd be so against this. You always talk about me needing to settle down … not that I'm settling down, but I would have thought you, of all people, would be happy to see me dating." She locked her eyes on his. "And he's not a rock star. He's a gospel singer."

Will sat his coffee cup on the table and eyed Maggie hard. "Maybe now, but he used to be a rock star. And now you're dating him. Listen, Sis, I would be happy if you were dating a doctor or CEO or lawyer, but a rock star? C'mon, let's be real. You're not exactly groupie material."

"I am not even going to ask what that was supposed to mean." Maggie crossed her arms.

Will leaned toward her. "It means that you're a professional. He's a, a—"

"A what?" She glared at him.

"You're *not* thinking this through."

"There really isn't anything to *think through*, Will." She pursed her lips. "Colin's a nice guy. I enjoy his company, and I think he enjoys mine. I'm not marrying the man. We're simply two people who like spending time together. We're friends, that's all."

Will took a deep breath. "You could get very hurt."

"I've been hurt before," Maggie said through clenched teeth, "but I survived then, and if it happens again, I'll survive again. Incidentally, he happens to be twenty-nine. He just looks younger. That's only a three-year difference. Hardly robbing the cradle. Need I remind you about the age difference between you and Val?"

"That's not the same thing," countered Will.

"How is it not?"

Will glowered at his sister. "This isn't about me and Val. I'm talking about you … getting hurt emotionally. He could be using you."

"For what?"

"I don't know, but you could be just another notch in his bedpost."

"You have got be kidding, right? Give me a little credit, Will."

"Well, it happens."

"You're becoming a bit melodramatic, don't you think? You must be watching too many soap operas in the afternoon.

116

You know, you ought to at least meet him before you pass judgment."

Will sat tight-lipped.

Maggie leaned back in her chair. "We are friends, Will. I am not a star-struck teenager. I have a career that I don't intend to just throw away to follow him around the country while he tours. I didn't even know who he was until a few weeks ago. Valerie knows more about him than I do, if you can believe what she's read in the tabloids."

Will threw up his hands. "My point exactly! You don't know him very well."

"I know him well enough." Determination sparked in Maggie's eyes.

"I don't like it, Maggie. If this guy is after you, he's going to have to go through me."

Maggie started to speak, but her pager went off. "The ER. I'll see you later. This conversation is not over, Will." She whirled around and headed for the emergency room.

As Maggie entered the emergency room, Valerie met her with a report on a firefighter who had been pulled out of a burning building after saving a trapped child. He had third degree burns on his face and hands, and was having difficulty breathing. Maggie passed through a line of worried firefighters and entered the treatment room.

"Hey, Doc," the firefighter said hoarsely. "How bad is it?

Maggie looked down at the man who, despite the severity of his injuries, did not complain of pain. His soot-covered face was swollen and his breathing was labored.

"Well, Joshua," she began, noting the name on the paramedic report, "I don't really know at this point, but we're going to do everything we can to make sure you come through this just fine."

She turned to Valerie. "Keep the oxygen at one hundred percent. Get a chest x-ray, ABG, CBC, and Chem-12. Oh, and make sure they do a carboxyhemoglobin test when they do the ABGs to check for carbon monoxide. Get Mark Denton. He's the best burn doc I know. Keep an eye on his respiratory status." She made several notations on the admission form, handed it to Valerie, and turned to her patient.

The firefighter managed a weak smile, then closed his eyes. Maggie proceeded to gently examine him. "I understand you went back into the building to rescue a child?"

"Yeah. Took a while to find her … she was hiding in a closet … ow!"

"I'm sorry."

"It's OK, Doc. I know you're just doing your job." His breathing was now shallow and he struggled to speak. "I had to … give her my mask, Doc … she was barely breathing."

Maggie nodded. He had removed his own oxygen mask and put it over the child's face to save her life. Now he was in critical condition, and in all probability would soon be fighting for his own life. She wished Dr. Denton would hurry.

"Try not to speak right now, Josh. I need you to conserve your energy." Maggie listened one more time to his lungs. Each breath produced small crackles and wheezes. She moved to allow the nurses to remove some of Josh's clothing before listening to his heart. A spasm of coughing interrupted her assessment.

"Denton's on his way," Valerie reported as Maggie leaned back over Josh to evaluate his cardiac status.

"Thanks, Val." She listened to the rapidly beating organ, but detected nothing abnormal. She made a few notations on the chart, and glanced up at the cardiac monitor.

"Hey, Maggie, what've you got?"

Maggie turned around, and sighed in relief when Dr. Mark Denton walked in. She handed him the chart and gave him a brief synopsis of Josh's history and current status.

"You're going to be just fine, Josh," Maggie said softly to the firefighter. "You're in the best hands possible." She looked up at Mark for confirmation and, when he nodded, she smiled faintly, then turned back to Josh. "I'll check in on you later."

As she walked out of the treatment room, a group of firefighters immediately surrounded her.

"He will be alright, won't he?"

"Yeah, Doc, he'll make it, right?

Maggie stopped and slowly looked at each man, her eyes meeting theirs before she spoke. "He's got the best burn doctor that I know, Mark Denton, taking care of him. If anyone can get him back on his feet, it's Dr. Denton." She paused for a moment, then smiled reassuringly. "It may take some time, but I believe Josh has a very good chance for a full recovery."

One by one, the men nodded their thanks and retreated to the waiting room.

Valerie walked over beside her sister-in-law. Her eyes followed the firefighters as they moved away from Maggie. "He will be alright, won't he?"

"I hope so, Val. I feel much better with Mark here, but it all depends on his lung status." They walked over to the nurses' station, and Maggie reviewed the patients' names listed on the board.

"Got anything else?" Maggie asked the clerk at the nurses' station.

"Possible cardiac is on its way in, otherwise, we're pretty quiet right now."

"I'll be in the lounge, Val. Please call me when it gets here." Maggie headed for a fresh cup of coffee.

The only other people in the lounge were two nurses sitting in the corner quietly conversing. Maggie poured herself a cup of coffee, and sat down on the sofa. She laid her head back and allowed her mind to wander to the day that she had met Scott Devereaux. Her heart still ached for the man who had once filled her world with so much joy. She was lost in thought when a nurse called her through the open lounge door.

"Dr. Devereaux?"

Maggie sat up.

"The cardiac has just arrived."

Maggie stepped out into the main hall of the emergency room, her coffee left steaming on the table beside the sofa.

Entering the treatment room to examine the potential heart patient, Maggie glanced up at the readings on the cardiac monitor. She saw that the heart rate was slightly accelerated, and the rhythm of the heart was regular. A nurse adjusted the intravenous line previously started in the field by the paramedics. Maggie picked up the bedside chart and read the name.

"Mr. Levin, I'm Dr. Devereaux. Can you tell me what brought you here today?" Maggie stood by the side of the bed, looking into the frightened eyes of her newest patient.

Howard Levin started to remove the oxygen mask.

"Let's leave that on. I can hear you just fine through the mask." Maggie noted his abnormally pale skin. She patted his hand, aware of the coolness and dampness of his fingers as they grasped hers.

"I wasn't doing anything, Doc. Really. I was watching some cartoon show with my grandson. He's the light of my life, Doc. Eight-years-old. My daughter was next door talking with Mrs. Cabrillo. It was some kind of superhero cartoon, I think. Anyway, I felt this awful pain in my chest, and it was hard to breathe. I didn't want to scare David, my grandson." He paused to take a breath.

"So I waited until my daughter, Natalia, came back in. She's studying to be a nurse. I didn't think it was anything because it got better, but Natalia wanted to be sure. Said she needed to call 9-1-1. I told her it wasn't necessary, but you know how daughters can be."

Maggie gently placed her hand on his shoulder. "How are you feeling now?"

"I've felt better, but then again, Doc, I've felt worse. You don't think it's my heart, do you? I eat right, and I walk every day. Natalia, she needs me." His eyes seemed to plead for something positive from Maggie.

"Well, Mr. Levin, I can't tell you too much right now that's very definitive, but my job is to make sure you're fine and healthy, and ready to help Natalia when she needs you. I'd like to examine you now if I may." She slipped the ends of the stethoscope into her ears.

"Absolutely, Doc." He laid his arms next to his side, allowing Maggie to listen to his chest.

Some irregularity in the heart rate. Is that an S4?

She listened carefully, but couldn't definitively ascertain whether or not what she heard was really an abnormal heart sound.

"Mr. Levin, I'd like to have a cardiologist examine you, if that's alright with you. Meanwhile, I'm going to order some lab tests that will help us determine exactly what's going on. Do you know what medicines you're taking?"

"More than I can remember. Natalia, she makes me carry a list." He fumbled in his pocket and produced a worn piece of paper. "Will this do?"

Thank goodness for daughters who take good care of their dads. "This is exactly what I need, Mr. Levin. I'll be back when the lab results return. Meanwhile, someone will be in here to take an EKG and a chest x-ray in a few minutes as well as to draw some blood. You just relax, but if you need anything, or you feel any pain, I want you to press this button. Either a nurse or I will come right in."

"Yes, yes, I will, Doc. Thank you so much. Will you talk to my daughter if she's here?"

Maggie patted his hand. "Yes, I will, and, after I speak with her, I'll send her in to sit with you."

"God bless you, Doc," Howard said as Maggie turned to leave. She hesitated a moment, then turned back to her patient.

"Thank you, Mr. Levin. You, too." As she left the room, she unfolded the wrinkled paper. *Digoxin, furosemide, potassium ... he has a history of cardiac problems.* She walked into a now crowded waiting area. "Family of Howard Levin?"

"I'm Natalia Parker, Howard's daughter." A slender, brown-haired woman stood up, worry etched all over her face. "How is he?"

"Let's sit over here," said Maggie as she directed Natalia to a secluded corner in the waiting room. "He's stable right now. We're doing some tests to determine if it's his heart."

"I wasn't sure if I should have called 9-1-1, but he looked awful, and he said he couldn't breathe well." Natalia pushed a loose strand of hair behind her ear.

"You did exactly right." Maggie placed her hand on Natalia's shoulder. "I understand you're a nursing student?"

The woman nodded, wiping her eyes with a tissue. "I'm in my second year."

Maggie held the young woman's hands in hers, and continued to speak softly but firmly. "You know the greatest danger from a heart attack is in the first two hours. You did the right thing. Your dad has several classic symptoms, but it still could be something else. That's why I'm ordering a

CBC, cardiac enzymes, ABGs, and a Chem-12 panel. Do you remember what these blood tests are for?"

"Yes, yes, I think so."

"Does your dad have any history of heart problems?"

"Yes, he has congestive heart failure, and a few years ago he had a heart attack. No one was with him then, and when I found him … I thought I was … going to lose him." Her voice broke. "He lives with me and my husband and son. He's on a lot of meds. I brought a list …"

"Yes, I saw it."

Natalia wiped another tear from her eye. "He has high blood pressure, too. I've tried to help him with his diet, but he's so … he's … stubborn at times."

Maggie squeezed her hand. "I think you're doing a great job with him. Now, it's our turn. We'll take very good care of him, too. I've asked a cardiologist to come and see him, but that may be a while. Would you like to go sit with him until the doctor arrives?"

When she nodded, Maggie led her to her father's bedside, and then returned to the nurses' station.

"Dr. Devereaux, patient in three," came a voice from behind her.

Maggie turned around. "No rest for the weary, Claire?"

"Not around this place."

As Maggie walked toward room three, she stifled a yawn. She passed through the curtains to find a nervous young man holding the hand of a wide-eyed young woman with a head full of blonde ringlets.

"Hello, I'm Dr. Devereaux. What seems to be the problem?"

"I think she's hypoglycemic or diabetic or something like that," stated the man moving out of Maggie's way. The young woman looked over at the man and smiled weakly.

"And you are …" Maggie scanned the chart for a name.

"Greg Brockman, Joy's husband." He extended his hand to Maggie.

"Nice to meet you, Mr. Brockman." Maggie shook his hand, and then turned her attention to the patient. "Have you ever been diagnosed as diabetic?"

"Uh-uh," answered Joy, shaking her head. "But Greg says I have all the symptoms."

"Yeah. I looked it up on the Internet. She's classic." He reached over to pat his wife's hand. "She's really been sick, and for a long time, too."

Oh boy. The Internet. Too much information, too little relevance.

"I see. Joy, can you tell me about these symptoms?"

Greg responded, "She gets sick to her stomach and throws up. Almost every day. Then she starts to feel better. She gets real tired, too. Y'know, what I mean?"

Maggie turned her attention to Greg. "I think so. You're very informative."

He smiled knowingly and nodded.

Maggie turned back to the woman. "When did this start?"

"Well, actually about—"

"Maybe a few weeks ago," interjected Greg.

If he doesn't let her answer, I'm going to throw him out of this room!

"Any fever or cough?"

"No," Joy answered, her body trembling. "I just feel sick all the time."

"Have you seen your regular doctor?" asked Maggie as she made some notes on the chart.

"No," replied Greg. "We used some herbal stuff that I read about on the 'Net, but that didn't really help."

Please shut up, just once.

"So, what made you come in today?"

"She just seems to be getting worse, and this morning she was throwing up, and well, I couldn't just not do anything." Greg hung his head. "I had to bring her in."

"I understand. Joy, let me check you over, then I'll order a few tests and we'll see what we can find out. Hopefully, we'll know something very soon."

After completing her exam, Maggie stepped outside and walked over to the nurses' station. She set the chart down and stood quietly thinking.

"Something wrong, Dr. Devereaux?"

"Oh, I'm sorry, Claire. I didn't mean to ignore you. I just have a hunch. Can you get a portable ultrasound up here? I think I may want to check something out after I get those lab results back."

"Sure thing. No problem." Claire picked up the phone and called radiology.

As soon as the lab tests returned, Maggie rolled the portable ultrasound machine next to Joy's bed.

"What's that for?" asked Greg. He sat next to his wife and squeezed her hand.

Maggie lifted Joy's gown to expose her abdomen. She squirted some water soluble lubricant on her skin and placed the transducer probe on her belly. She began to move it around.

"This is an ultrasound machine. It uses sound waves to help create images that can give me information about what might be causing Joy's discomfort."

Greg leaned over to Joy. "Oh, yeah. I read about this, sweetheart, on the web."

Of course.

Joy smiled, admiring her husband. Despite her irritation at Greg for monopolizing the conversation, the devotion of the young couple for each other touched Maggie, and she hoped the ultrasound would verify the results of the HCG blood test. She kept her eyes on the ultrasound display screen.

"Ah," said Maggie, finding what she was looking for. She turned the display toward the couple. "Mr. and Mrs. Brockman, can you see this right here?" She pointed out a pale image on the screen.

Greg's brow furrowed. "Yes. What is it?"

"That is the source of the nausea and fatigue."

"Can it be cured?" asked Greg, worry crossing his face.

"Yes, it can. In about seven and a half months." She pointed again to the image. "This is your baby."

"What?" Greg nearly shouted. "Our baby?" He leaned over and stared at the screen. "Are you sure, Doc? A baby? We're going to have a baby? Sweetheart! We're going to have a baby!"

Greg moved closer to Joy and laced his fingers through hers. Together, they stared at the tiny image on the ultrasound screen. Maggie described what they saw on the monitor, and Greg slowly got out of his chair and walked over to the screen. He reached out his hand and gently touched the image.

"What's that?" he asked in a whisper.

"That little fluttering is your child's heart beating."

"Is it a boy or a girl?" asked Greg, almost reverently.

"It's too soon to tell, but at about sixteen weeks or so, you can probably find out. You need to set up an appointment with an obstetrician. I'll get you the number of one of our OB's on staff. Give him a call tomorrow. I'm sorry but I'm not comfortable giving you anything for the nausea, since you're in the first trimester, the first three months of your pregnancy. I'll let your obstetrician handle that, OK?"

"Sure, Doc. We understand," Greg nodded vigorously, his eyes moist. "Will we be able to go home today?"

"Absolutely. I'll write the discharge orders, and I'll get you the name of the obstetrician. Make sure you call him."

"We will, Doc, and thanks, thanks so much!"

"My pleasure and congratulations to you both." The Brockmans were holding each other and crying when Maggie left the room.

I'm going to cry myself in a minute. They are so sweet. She stopped just outside of their room and turned back to take one more look at the couple, breathing out a deep sigh.

Scott and I, we could've had that.

She slowly walked to the nurses' station and wrote the discharge orders before heading for the staff lounge.

"Dr. Devereaux?"

Maggie turned to see Claire walking toward her.

"I have the lab results for Levin."

Maggie scanned the numbers on the paper. "Looks like our Mr. Levin may have had an MI. Can you get a bed for me in CCU?"

She headed directly for his room. As she entered, she saw Natalia sitting quietly, holding her father's hand as he snored softly into the oxygen mask. The only other sound was the steady beeping of the cardiac monitor.

"How are you doing, Natalia?" asked Maggie as she stopped near the foot of the bed.

"Pretty good. How's my dad doing?"

Howard's eyes fluttered open. "Hey Doc, did I pass?"

Maggie moved to the side of the bed and put her hand on his shoulder. "Unfortunately, Mr. Levin, the test results indicate that you probably had a mild heart attack. It's a good thing you're here. Your daughter did just what she was trained to do. I'm having you moved to the cardiac care unit, and I'm asking Dr. Eliot to take charge of your case. He's one of the best cardiologists we have on staff here. You will be in excellent hands, and with the proper care and treatment, you should be just fine."

Natalia glanced up at Maggie, a veil of tears threatening to spill over onto her cheeks. "Thank you so much, Dr. Devereaux. My dad, he's … I love him so much."

"I know, Natalia," Maggie knelt down to look directly into the young woman's eyes. "He'll be fine. You got him here in plenty of time. There'll be some more tests, you know that. Based on those results, a plan of treatment will be made. You'll be there to make sure your father follows the after-care regime, and he should be around for many, many years to enjoy you and his precious grandson."

The tears finally fell, and Natalia leaned over to hug Maggie. "Thank you so much, Doctor. I'm sorry, it's just that—"

"No need to apologize. If it were my father, I'd feel exactly like you." She turned to Howard. "You're lucky to have such a devoted daughter."

"Don't I know it, Doc, don't I know it."

Maggie left the room and walked over to the nurses' station. "Did we get Mr. Levin a room?" She picked up a chart and flipped through it to the physician's pages.

Claire looked up at Maggie. "Yes, they'll be down in a few minutes to transfer him. Eliot's on his way."

Maggie nodded. "Wonderful. How are the Brockmans doing?" She finished signing off some orders and replaced the chart.

"They just left, smiling from ear to ear, I might add."

Maggie smiled, then looked up at the assignment board, noting no new additions. She headed for the staff lounge to sit down for a few minutes before the next influx of patients. She plopped down on the worn sofa and stifled a yawn, tired, but satisfied. The good news she delivered to the Brockmans elated Maggie.

I love my job! No matter how bad it gets, these days make up for them all!

She closed her eyes just as the door opened, and Valerie stuck her head in.

"Sorry, Mags, but we need you in two."

But then again … Maggie shook her head in resignation as she took one final sip of her freshly poured coffee before walking out of the staff lounge.

CHAPTER ELEVEN

"YOU'RE NOT *SERIOUS*, are you?" asked Will, his voice escalating.

"Why does every conversation about Colin end up with you questioning my sanity?" Maggie jammed her hands on her hips.

Will shook his head. "Maybe if you didn't come up with such crazy ideas, I wouldn't be doubting your mental status."

Maggie took a deep breath and glared at her brother from across his dining room table. She drummed her fingers lightly, trying to control her irritation.

"Just exactly what are you concerned about? This didn't bother you when I went with Scott the first time."

Will shrugged. "That was different."

"Really? How so?"

"Scott wasn't—"

"Wasn't what? A singer? A former patient? What? What exactly do you have against Colin?" Her eyes bore into his.

Will crossed his arms and fought to keep his voice controlled. "I don't want you to get hurt. I don't want to see that happen."

"Really, Will. I am a big girl, besides, Colin and I, well, we're just friends. And I think I know him fairly well. It's been almost three months."

He cocked his head. "Three whole months? You think that's enough time to get to know someone?"

Maggie breathed in deeply and held it for a moment, then slowly exhaled. Her response was steady, but firm. "It was for you and Valerie, remember? Besides, Colin and I are becoming good friends, and I think he ought to know about the things I'm passionate about—including Santa Molina. It's just like it was with Scott. We'll have separate cabins, besides Ryan is there. I can't have a better chaperone than a preacher."

Will clenched his fists. "I don't like it."

Maggie glared at her brother again. "You don't like it? You can't even give me one substantial reason for him not to go with me."

"It's awfully impulsive."

"Impulsive? Are you worried I'll run off and get married?"

Will didn't answer, nor did he look at Maggie.

"Will Garrett, if this wasn't so pathetic, it would be comical." Maggie laughed. "Marriage? Me? You have got to be kidding. How many times do I need to tell you that we are just friends?"

"What's so ridiculous about it? He's good looking, rich, and lives a glamorous lifestyle. You're beautiful, successful, and quite a catch, I might add."

"I cannot believe what I'm hearing. Do you really think I'd give up my career to marry Colin and move to England?"

"I just think you should take it slow."

"I really don't think you need to caution me on how to live my life, Will. Besides there is nothing to take slow. Friends, got it? We're just friends."

Will stood up and held out his palms. "I'm not sure you're thinking straight, Maggie. Inviting Colin to go with you could be sending the wrong message."

"Wrong message? Just what exactly would that message be?"

At that moment, the front door opened, and Valerie entered with two sacks of Chinese take-out. She began pulling the containers out of the bags and setting them on the dining room table between Maggie and Will.

"I hope you're hungry, you two. I couldn't make up my mind, so I bought everything that looked good."

Neither Will nor Maggie spoke.

Valerie's eyes moved quickly from her husband to her sister-in-law.

"What's up, guys?"

Maggie kept her eyes on Will, her lips drawn in a thin line. "He doesn't think I should invite Colin to go with me to Santa Molina at the end of the month."

Will glanced at his wife. "I don't think it's a good idea, Val. She hardly knows him."

"I don't know if that's entirely correct, Will, but go on," said Valerie.

Will's eyes darted from Val's face to Maggie's. "What does that mean? 'Not entirely correct'? Just how well do you know him, Maggie?"

"Do not speak to me in that tone of voice, Will Garrett," cautioned Maggie.

"Or what?" challenged Will.

"OK, you two, calm down," said Valerie, turning to her husband. "Will, tell me why you think it's a bad idea to invite Colin."

He sighed. "I don't know why I bother; she's going to do what she wants anyway."

Valerie reached out, took her husband's hand, and said softly, "Will, your sister is thirty-two-years-old. Don't you think she's entitled to do what she wants in her life?"

He shook his head. "Not when she's acting stupid." He closed his eyes and rubbed his forehead.

"Stupid? You're calling me stupid?" Maggie's eyes flashed with anger.

"As a matter of fact—"

"Will, hush!" commanded Valerie. "Maggie, what's this all about? You're inviting Colin to go to Santa Molina?"

Maggie crossed her arms. "I'd told Colin about Santa Molina a while back, and he said that it sounded like someplace he'd like to see someday. Then a few days ago, Ryan called and asked if I'd be willing to come down again to help out sometime between now and the end of the summer. Money's been tight for him, and he needs a doctor to cover for a few weeks. So, instead of paying for one, he asked if I might be able to come down and help.

"I haven't asked Colin about coming on this particular trip, but I thought I might ask him the next time we have dinner, and see if he's interested in going with me. It's really not that big of a deal."

Valerie looked her sister-in-law directly in the eyes. "It is to Will, Mags, and you need to understand that, too. He cares about you, as do I, but he looks at things a bit differently than we do." She patted Maggie's hand. "You two need to resolve this without coming to blows. Now, Will, Mags, can you two discuss this civilly while I go get some plates and forks?" She stood up and waited for them both to nod their heads before exiting into the kitchen area.

"Maggie," began Will, "you need to think this through."

"Don't you think I have, Will? Don't you think I've thought about what could happen? But it won't. He just wants to be friends. I just want to be friends. What Colin and I have right now is perfect. We are two people who happen to enjoy one another's company. No strings. Besides, eventually he goes back to England; I stay here. Maybe we share a phone call now and then, but it ends there."

"I'm sorry. I know it's really not my business, but, it's just that—just be careful, OK?"

A small smile creased Maggie's lips. "I promise I'll be careful. Colin is a very nice guy. He really is."

"Maybe. I guess I don't have the opportunity to ask everyone about him, like I did Scott, so I guess that makes me a bit nervous."

"You checked up on Scott?"

"Yeah." Will chuckled. "I wanted to make sure he was good enough for you." He winked at Maggie. "He was."

"Yes, he definitely was."

Will took a deep breath and sighed. "It's just that I love you, Sis."

"I know."

Valerie entered and glanced at them. "That's better. You ready to eat?"

"Yeah, I'm starved," said Will as he scooped a large portion of chow mein onto his plate. The three filled their plates with food and sat on padded chairs around the circular glass table.

"Maybe you ought to invite Colin over for dinner, and we could spend some time getting to know him," suggested Valerie as she took a bite of her egg roll. "That might help Will a bit."

"So he can be interrogated by my well-meaning brother?" Maggie chuckled. "That'll be the day." She picked up a pair of chopsticks.

"I think it's a good idea," said Will between bites. "I would feel better if I could meet him before you went to Santa Molina. And I *promise* I'll be nice."

Maggie raised an eyebrow. "You think I'm going to believe you?"

"I will be. Besides, what do you have to lose? I already don't like the guy. It can't get any worse than that."

Valerie punched her husband in the arm. "Will! How can you dislike someone you haven't met?"

Will threw up his hands and laughed. "He's after my sister, that's why."

Maggie threw a fortune cookie and hit Will on the forehead.

"Hey, what was that for?"

"That's for being an idiot," said Maggie as she popped a piece of sesame chicken into her mouth. "Valerie, what on earth did you see in this man that compelled you to marry him? Was it a moment of temporary insanity?"

Valerie laughed. "Ah, c'mon, Mags, he does have a good side."

"She's right. I do have a good side."

"Really? Do you keep it in hiding until I'm gone? You have to promise you'll have an open mind when you meet him, or no dinner."

"I will do my best. I promise."

"OK. I'll ask him over Monday night. Will that work for you both?"

"Works for me," stated Valerie, sipping her diet soda.

Will nodded. "I'll make it work for me."

Colin still enjoyed his early morning jogs along the beach, despite associating them with his bout of pericarditis. Maggie convinced him the two weren't related and he believed her, so he still rose early and jogged a couple of miles along the shore. The only sounds that he usually heard were the occasional cries of the gulls and the soothing repetitive pounding of the waves against the sand. The solitude gave him ample opportunity to think and pray, and he relished the time alone with the Lord. This morning was no exception, but he found that even after returning home, he was preoccupied with his feelings about Maggie.

I can't get her out of my mind. I keep postponing going home so I can see her. I am so afraid of falling in love with her, and yet I want her in my life so badly.

He poured himself a glass of water, and stepped out onto the deck. Leaning against the railing of his patio, he watched a group of wet-suited surfers tackle the crashing waves of the Pacific Ocean. He ran his fingers through his blonde hair, lightened even more by the constant exposure to the sun.

This album is almost finished. What do I do? Stay? Go back to London?

Squinting his eyes, he watched a lone pelican soar near the top of the waves before it dove into the surf and popped back out, floating on top of the water. Taking another sip of water, he set the glass down on the railing, and, leaning on his elbows, began to talk to God.

"Lord, I really need some help here. I like Maggie, I really do, but I know we're not on the same page with You. I love being with her, but I know I shouldn't get involved with someone who isn't saved. I don't understand why You let our paths cross, or why You've let me develop such strong feelings for her if it's never going anywhere. Father, please give me the strength to trust You and submit to Your will. I know it's the best way."

He gazed out to the ocean, seeing the same turmoil in the waves that he felt in his heart. The struggle within his soul was nearly overwhelming and threatened to drown him.

"I'm starting to understand what Paul meant when he said 'For the good that I would I do not: but the evil which I would not, that I do.' This is so hard, Lord. I, I think I'm falling in love with her." His petition became an ardent plea, and his voice broke as he prayed.

"Help her find You, Lord. Your Word says that You're not willing that any should perish, but that all should come to repentance. That means Maggie, too, so I'm claiming that for her, Lord, please. In the name of Your precious Son, Jesus, I pray, amen."

Colin stood up and looked out over the water. He took another deep breath just as his cell phone rang. Pulling it from his pocket, he looked at the display: Maggie.

He cast his eyes upward and whispered, "What are you doing to me, Lord?" He let the phone ring several times before putting it to his ear. He tried to answer as cheerfully as he could.

"Hi, Maggie, what's up?" Colin turned his back to the ocean, leaned on the railing, and put one foot up on the deck rail. "Dinner to meet the family? Sounds serious," teased Colin as he tried to sound nonchalant.

On the other end, Maggie laughed. "My brother is a bit overprotective, and he's got some very interesting preconceived notions about famous rock singers. So, he'd like to get to know you."

"That doesn't sound like it's in my favor." He stood up straight. "So what do you suggest I do to win over your brother?" Overhead, a gull soared on the sea breeze casting a fleeting shadow across Colin's face.

"Just be yourself. There's no way he can't like you."

"Hmm, I think I can handle that. After all, that's how I won you over, right?" He heard Maggie laugh softly.

"Will Monday night work for you?"

Colin hesitated for a moment, hoping this was God's leading. "Yeah, it'll be fine. I'll see you then." He hung up the phone and looked to the sky. "It will be fine, right?"

Monday evening came quickly, and Maggie felt her nervousness intensify as the dinner hour neared. She examined her dining room table once more. Four place settings sat atop a lace tablecloth. In the center was a vase with a small spray of miniature pink roses. On each side of the vase was a small jasmine scented tea candle. She lit both and stood back, smiling, satisfied with the results. Although it was still fifteen minutes before anyone was expected to arrive, her doorbell rang.

Let it be him.

She opened the door, and her smile broadened. Looking very relaxed, Colin wore an open collared light green shirt with a pair of denim jeans.

"I thought I'd come by a bit early in case you needed some help." He held out a single yellow rose for her.

"You are always so thoughtful. Thank you." She held the flower to her nose and inhaled deeply. "This is lovely! Come on in. Actually, I think I'm ready … except for the garlic bread, but I'll wait on that until Will and Val get here."

Colin followed Maggie into the kitchen area.

"Smells nice in here. So, now you're a doctor *and* a cook?" asked Colin as he spooned a bit of marinara sauce out of a simmering pot. "Now, this is good."

Maggie smiled and imitated Colin's intonations. "So you're a singer *and* a food critic?"

Colin grinned. "Oh, yeah. I'm a man of many talents." He returned the spoon to its cradle. "Are you sure there's nothing I can do?" At that moment the doorbell rang again.

Maggie raised an eyebrow and looked at Colin. "You game to answer the door?"

"Ooh ... sending the lamb to its slaughter? Sure, I can handle that."

Maggie watched him head toward the front door, listening for the dialogue as she grabbed the butter and garlic salt for the bread she hoped Valerie had remembered to bring.

Please let my brother like him!

"Hi there," said Colin, offering his hand. "You must be Will. I've heard a lot about you. I'm Colin."

Clad in a light blue polo shirt and khaki slacks, Will shook Colin's hand, slightly surprised at seeing him and not Maggie. "Nice to meet you. This is my wife, Valerie, but I believe you two have already met."

"It's good to see you again." Valerie's hazel eyes sparkled, and her dark brown ponytail swayed against her pale yellow sundress as she carried a loaf of French bread into the house. "I'm going to see if Maggie needs any help," she said as she walked toward the kitchen. "You're on your own, Will."

Will frowned as he watched his wife disappear into the kitchen. He crossed his arms as he turned back to face Colin.

So, this is the guy. This is going to be a long night.

"Maggie tells me you're a singer," Will said as he moved to the ivory leather sofa while Colin chose the matching loveseat opposite Will. "How's that going for you?"

"Pretty good, really." Colin swung an arm along the back of the loveseat. "It pays the bills."

"Maggie says you sing religious music?"

"Yeah, traditional mainly or my own compositions."

"Didn't you start out as a rock and roll singer?"

"Well, actually more like pop."

Will shifted in his seat. "Where exactly does one go to school to learn how to sing pop?"

Colin shrugged his shoulders. "Well, I don't know about other singers, but most of my training came from the Royal Academy of Music ... and Julliard."

"Is that so? What kind of training do they offer there for rock and roll singers?"

Colin thought for a moment. "I don't believe they have a program for rock and roll. I studied classical piano and voice."

Will's eyes widened, but he quickly composed himself. "Is that so? Graduate?"

"Yes." Colin said slowly, his eyes never leaving Will's face. "From both."

"I hear Julliard is a good school."

"I like to think so." Colin leaned forward, elbows on his knees and fingers interlocked. He looked directly at Will and asked pointedly, "Exactly what do you want to know about me and Maggie?"

What am I supposed to say to that? Fine. He asked. I'll answer.

"I want to know your intentions. I want to know that you're not going to hurt her."

"My intentions?" Colin arched his eyebrows. "My intentions are to be a good friend to her and enjoy our friendship. I have absolutely no intention of hurting Maggie. She is a sweet, intelligent, beautiful lady. I respect and admire her.

I'm just hoping to get to know her better. We're ... we're just friends.

"I honestly don't know where this is going, that's in God's hands, but I promise you I am not trying to string her along. I don't have a hidden agenda. I will admit that she means an awful lot to me, but whatever happens ..." Colin saw Maggie and Valerie enter the dining area with a large platter of spaghetti, a huge bowl of salad, and a basket of freshly made garlic bread. He stood up quickly.

"Do you need some help?"

Maggie smiled warmly at Colin. "No, I think we've got it all covered. You two can join us in a moment if you're ready."

Will watched the nonverbal exchange between Colin and Maggie.

Just friends, huh? Not a chance!

The dinner went well with the help of Valerie and Maggie, who guided the conversation to include topics of interest to both Will and Colin. By the end of the meal, all four were comfortably talking about everything from food to entertainment to travel. At the end of the evening, Will shook hands again with Colin. Keeping the conversation between them, he said, "She is my sister, Colin. I will do whatever I have to do to protect her."

Colin looked squarely at him. "I understand. I promise I won't hurt her."

Will returned his stare. "Make sure you don't."

Valerie gave Colin a quick kiss on the cheek, and whispered into his ear, "I think you two are perfect for each other."

Colin's eyes widened, but he didn't say a word as he watched them leave.

"That wasn't so bad," said Colin while loading the dishwasher. "By any chance was your brother a hit man for the mob before he became a doctor?"

Maggie giggled as she continued to tuck away the extra food from dinner into the fridge. "At least you survived the scrutiny."

Colin chuckled. "I suppose it could've been worse."

"Oh, yeah," said Maggie, nodding her head. "He could've shot you."

Colin straightened up to face Maggie. "Then I'm glad it went so well." He leaned against the counter.

"You and me both. Too much paperwork when you have to work on a gunshot wound."

Colin laughed heartily. "Your concern for my well-being is overwhelming."

"I'm a doctor, remember? That's my job!" She wiped off the counter, and tried to hide the nervousness that was beginning to escalate within her.

Tonight went well, so how do I ask him to go with me to Santa Molina? And how do I ask him to go without it seeming like I ... well, like I like him. Maybe he won't even want to go. Maybe he won't even be here. Maybe ... maybe I should just ask him.

"Colin, I need to ask you something." Maggie wiped her hands on the dish towel. "Can we talk?"

"Sure. Sounds serious," said Colin apprehensively. "This isn't going to be another inquisition, is it?"

"No. I do want to ask you something, but I don't even know where to begin." Maggie leaned against the kitchen counter opposite him.

"How about starting at the beginning? It can't really be all that bad, can it?"

Maggie shook her head. "I don't think it's bad at all ... unless you say 'no.'"

"Then I won't."

"Won't what?"

"Say 'no.'"

He's trying to make this easier for me, but I think it's just getting harder. I need to just say it.

"It's about Santa Molina. I'm going to be leaving to go there in a couple of weeks, and I was wondering ..." She glanced down at the ceramic floor. "I'm sorry. I didn't think this would be so difficult. I even planned what I was going to say." She took another deep breath and clasped her hands in front of her.

Colin waited patiently.

"I'm going to Santa Molina next month—"

"I believe you mentioned that already," he said with a grin.

"Yes, I did." A small smile touched her lips. "I think I told you about the clinic and the work that Scott's brother does there, right?"

Colin nodded.

"And you said that you'd maybe like to visit one day."

"Yes."

"So, I was wondering if, um, you'd consider ... coming with me on this trip to help me and Ryan. It would really be a wonderful experience. You'd love the kids, I mean, there's so much to do there. Ryan's having trouble financing a doctor, and I said I'd help out for a couple of weeks." She took a quick breath. "I realize I'm rambling. It's just that ... I've been thinking about this for quite a while, and I would really like for you to consider coming with me. The only thing it would cost is plane fare because Ryan would pick us up, and we could stay in the cabins there. All the food is provided, and—"

"Maggie ... money really isn't a problem." He paused and studied her face. "Are you really sure you'd like me to

go with you?" Another moment of silence passed. "Is ...
Will ... OK with this?"

"Yes, I really would, and Will has his reservations, but ..."
Maggie sighed. She gazed into his steady blue eyes, and then
finally said, "I think it would be wonderful if you came."
She lowered her eyes and added softly, "I would really love
to have you with me."

Of course, I want to go, but, Lord please, I don't understand.
Colin's heart was telling him to go, but his head was
cautious. He needed to know this was God's will, and he
had to have total peace about joining Maggie. Instantly, a
verse of Scripture came to mind: *Trust in the Lord with all
thine heart and lean not unto thine own understanding. In all
thy ways acknowledge Him, and He shall direct thy paths.*

Maggie glanced up at Colin and made one final plea.
"You'd love Ryan, and maybe the trip would give you an
opportunity to minister to the people in Santa Molina."

Colin smiled. Maggie already knew how to get to his
heart. Sharing the gospel, spending time with her. His heart
was winning the battle.

*How can I be sure going to Santa Molina is God's will and
not mine? What could I possibly do to help down there? I'm
not a doctor, and Maggie's going to work in a clinic.*

Colin knew it would be too easy to rationalize going
simply for the opportunity to spend more time with Maggie.
He quickly offered another unspoken prayer to his Savior.
*Lord, help me to know this is You and not me because You
know I'd say 'yes' in a heartbeat, and it wouldn't be because
I'm feeling particularly spiritual right now. Please, show me
Your will. Help me to know it's undeniably You, and for the
cause of Christ.*

Maggie looked directly into Colin's eyes. "And there's one more thing."

"There's more?"

Maggie bit her lip. "Maybe, we could find some time where maybe ... you could help me understand your faith more."

Colin froze.

How do I say no to that, Lord? Isn't this an open door to share Christ with her? Isn't that what I've been asking for?

"Hmmm, can you get me the dates so I can clear my calendar?"

Maggie stared at Colin wide-eyed.

"Maggie? The dates?"

She blinked and she shook her head quickly. "Oh, sorry. Of course, I can get you the dates ... I just didn't expect ... I have them here on my calendar." She opened her purse and grabbed her personal organizer, while Colin pulled out his cell phone.

"... Hold on a minute, Gary," Colin said into the phone. He looked at Maggie. "When?"

He repeated the dates to Gary. "Yeah. No, not really. I think so. That works for me. Yeah. I'll see you tomorrow. Thanks." Colin replaced his cell phone in a pocket. "I'm clear to go." His grinned filled his face.

"Really? Just like that?" Maggie asked, shaking her head. "Wow! I need a manager."

"Well, they do have their moments." They both stepped away from the counter.

"I've only got a few finishing touches left on the album," explained Colin, "and that should be done before we leave. After that, I'm yours."

Suddenly Maggie's eyes sparkled and her smile broadened. "You'll love it in Santa Molina, Colin." She waved her hands around as she spoke. "The people there are so sweet, and Ryan, well, he is such a wonderful man. I know you two will hit it off. I can look into the flight arrangements, and if you have no particular preferences, I'll go ahead and book the tickets." Colin held up a finger to silence her.

"Well, actually, I do have a few preferences. Would you mind if I arranged the flight?"

Maggie tilted her head. "Are you sure? Oh, of course … I forget. I'm traveling with a celebrity. Of course, you'll want to make the arrangements. Just let me know the details, and we'll settle up later. I'll let Ryan know when we'll be there, so he can pick us up."

Colin nodded. "No problem. I'll get the information to you by tomorrow, OK?"

"Absolutely!" Maggie's voice was almost melodic. "I can't wait to call Ryan and tell him the good news."

Colin smiled. The 'good news' was exactly what he hoped Maggie would hear and embrace *before* he fell completely and hopelessly in love with her.

CHAPTER TWELVE

O N THEIR RIDE to the airport, Maggie explained as much as she could to Colin about her work at the clinic in Santa Molina. He tried to listen attentively, but found his mind drifting to the surprise he had planned for her.

As they pulled into the airport parking lot, Maggie became more enthusiastic about the clinic in the Mexican town and Ryan's ministry, and Colin saw a new side of her. *She is so beautiful! Her whole face lights up when she speaks. I could listen to her for hours.* Pulling up to the terminal, he jumped out and ran around the car to open the door for her.

Looking up at the terminal and finding no airline name except for a small shuttle service, Maggie looked at Colin with one eyebrow raised. "What airline did you book us on?"

As he unloaded their luggage from the car, Colin spoke briefly to an airport employee, who took their luggage, and then he turned to Maggie, "I'm sorry, love. What did you say?"

Maggie put her hands on her hips and stared at Colin suspiciously.

"Oh, well, I have sort of a surprise for you," said Colin as he offered her his arm. "I hope you won't be upset with me."

Maggie poked him in the chest, feigning irritation. "You know I am not a fan of surprises."

"I know. I was hoping you'd forgive me this one time because if you don't, it'll be a very long flight." He shrugged his shoulders and held up his hands as if to indicate he had no other option. "It's one of those surprises that you have to accept no matter what."

Once in the terminal, Maggie glanced around. Her eyes darted from one end of the terminal to the other.

"Where are we, Colin?"

"Los Angeles International Airport, remember? We're going to Santa Molina?" replied Colin. "Trust me. We're heading toward our plane."

In a few minutes, they were standing on the tarmac in front of a beautifully streamlined private jet.

"We're flying on that? This is the surprise? How in the world did you manage it?" Maggie stared at the aircraft in front of her.

"Well ... I did tell you I had a few special preferences. Plus, we can get there in less time than a commercial flight, fly non-stop, and have lots of leg room." He winked at her and grinned.

"How in the world did you manage this? It had to cost a fortune," said Maggie as she climbed the stairs into the plane.

A pilot met them at the top of the plane's stairs.

"Good morning, Mr. Grant. Dr. Devereaux. Welcome aboard."

"Impressive," whispered Maggie to Colin as she entered the fuselage of the plane. Maggie gasped as she gazed around at the accommodations. Colin was speaking with the pilot, but turned around when he heard her muted, "Oh, my goodness."

"You OK, love?"

Maggie nodded without moving her eyes from the plush interior of the plane.

Colin shook the pilot's hand. "Thanks, John. Everything ready?"

"Yes, sir. Everything's on board and ready to go."

"Terrific. How about the weather?"

"Couldn't be better."

"Great," replied Colin as he followed Maggie into the plane. "Let's get seated, love." He guided her to her seat, and then sat opposite her after making sure she was buckled securely.

"Aren't there any other passengers?"

"No. Just us."

Maggie scowled as she watched Colin settle in his seat. *I hope she's not really mad at me.* "What?" he asked, looking at Maggie. "What's wrong?"

"When are you going to explain this to me?" She crossed her arms in front of her.

Now that's not a good sign.

"Explain what? The plane?"

Maggie just stared at him.

I think she's really mad at me.

Finally, she spoke. "Why in the world did you charter a private jet?"

"Because I told you I had some preferences, remember?"

"What kind of preferences?"

"I feel safer when my own pilot is flying." He crossed his legs and settled back in his seat.

"*Your* pilot?"

"Um ... hmm. Comfortable?"

"Is … this … *your* … plane, too?"

"Yes."

The plane began to accelerate on the runway.

"Oh my," whispered Maggie, looking out the window. "Tell me you're not a millionaire."

"OK. I'm not a millionaire."

"Really?"

"You told me to say that."

"Colin—"

"It's not that bad, Maggie, and it doesn't change anything, does it? I'm still me."

Maggie just stared out the window.

She's mad at me.

He leaned forward in his seat. "*Does it?*"

Maggie breathed out a sigh. "No It's just very … very … unexpected. Why didn't you tell me?"

"Tell you what? The balance in my bank account?"

Maggie frowned. "Of course not. You could have mentioned that you owned your own plane."

"It's not really something that comes up in conversation. Besides, you never asked me. Are you comfortable?"

"Colin Grant you are impossible! If I had something to throw at you, I would! And yes, I am quite comfortable, thank you."

"Why are you mad at me? What did I do? You told me I could book our flights, and I did. The scheduling was exactly what we needed, and I knew that the accommodations would be excellent, so I made the arrangements. I wanted to surprise you."

A smile lit across her lips. "That you did, but really, a private jet? You didn't think to tell me we'd be flying on a *private* jet? And yours, for that matter? And I'm not mad."

Colin rolled his eyes. "I thought you'd handle it better than this."

Maggie's eyes narrowed. "I am handling this fine."

"You could've fooled me."

"You've got to admit it is a little bit ... unorthodox."

Colin held up his palms. "What? Finding out I own a plane? Lots of people own planes."

"Maybe in your circle of friends, but most of mine drive cars. It's kind of a novelty to know someone who has their own jet. Do you fly, too?" A hint of sarcasm rang in her voice.

"No. I'm not a pilot. Would you like something to drink?"

"Are you going to get it, or do you have a flight attendant hidden somewhere?"

Colin grinned. "No, no flight attendant. I'm not that rich!"

Maggie's eyes softened. "Could've fooled me." She uncrossed her arms and leaned back in her seat. "OK, the shock is wearing off, but next time you plan a surprise for me—don't!"

"Wow, I really thought you would handle this better."

"I think I handled it pretty well, considering it's my first private jet ride with a celebrity who's filthy rich."

"I never said I was 'filthy rich.'"

"You didn't have to. Barely rich people drive Ferrari's and live in Beverly Hills. Filthy rich people own their own planes." Maggie laughed softly. "I will admit, this is an awfully nice way to travel. I guess it will be to my advantage to have a friend who owns a plane."

"It definitely comes in handy at times." Colin relaxed in his seat.

The plane easily soared above the local cloud cover, turning south toward Mexico and the small town of Santa Molina.

The city of Veracruz was home to the closest major airport to Santa Molina, and the plane arrived there in the mid-afternoon. Nestled in the foothills of the Eastern Sierra Madre Mountains on the shores of the Gulf of Mexico, the Mexican city had been a crossroad for various cultures since the early 1600s.

Disembarking at the terminal designated for private planes, Colin and Maggie meandered through the airport, finding their way to the exit without too much difficulty. A refreshing ocean breeze filtered through the airport waiting area, and it only took a moment for them to hear their names called out.

"Maggie! Colin! Welcome!" Ryan Devereaux rushed over to embrace Maggie. "It has been too long, my dear sister."

Colin watched the loving reunion between the pastor and Maggie.

"It is good to finally meet you, Colin," said Ryan warmly. He shook the singer's hand vigorously. "I am so thrilled that Maggie convinced you to come visit us. We can always use an extra hand at the church."

"It's good to be here, Pastor."

"Please, call me Ryan. I've heard a lot about you from Maggie."

Maggie slid into the center of the bench seat of the truck while the men loaded the luggage into the bed. She rode without speaking, choosing to listen to Ryan and Colin chat about their respective occupations. As the scenery changed from coastal to mountainous foothills and lush vegetation, the men's conversation faded into the background of Maggie's mind as she reminisced about the wonderful times she had shared with Scott in the small Mexican village.

I wonder what they'll think about me bringing another man with me.

As they pulled into the driveway leading up to the main area of the church, Maggie looked around the courtyard. The familiarity gave her tremendous peace, and she was eager to show Colin around the premises.

"Maggie, after you and Colin get settled in, we can all take a walk around, and I can show you what we've done since your last visit. I think you'll be very pleased with the additions to the clinic." Ryan motioned to a row of cabins they were approaching. "You know where you'll be staying. I'll take Colin to his cabin."

Maggie started to walk away from the men when a barefooted young boy, wearing only a pair of cut-off denim pants, ran up to her and grabbed her around the knees.

"*¡Doctora! ¡Doctora!*"

Maggie stooped down and hugged the little boy. "It is so good to see you, Miguel." She closed her eyes briefly, enjoying the embrace, then tousled his hair before standing up.

"*¿Quién es él?*" said the boy, pointing to Colin. The frown on his face hinted of disapproval.

"*Yo soy un amigo de la doctora,*" answered Colin, explaining that he was Maggie's friend.

Maggie's eyes widened. "You speak Spanish?"

Colin nodded. "A little. Two summers in Spain during high school. The dialect is a bit different, but hopefully it'll do while I'm here."

Ryan patted Colin on the back. "You're going to fit in just fine here, brother." He led Colin to his cabin, leaving Maggie with the young boy. She pulled a peppermint candy out of her pocket and handed it to Miguel.

"*Gracias, Doctora.*" Miguel cast one more quick glance at Colin and Ryan, then he scampered off. Maggie waved goodbye and headed to her cabin.

She pushed open the wooden door and noticed the cabin had recently been cleaned and aired out. She set her suitcase on the bed, opened it, and began to place her things in the appropriate places. After washing her face and changing into a pastel print sundress, Maggie went outside to look for Colin. She found him and Ryan sitting under a large leafed tree. Ryan was pointing to various buildings and explaining their uses.

Colin stood up as Maggie approached.

"All settled in?" he asked, motioning for her to sit beside him.

"For now. What are you two talking about?"

"I was telling Colin about the plans to add an assembly hall over there. It's just in the planning stages. We need to raise the money first, but as soon as that's done, we'll break ground. The clinic is almost finished, I think. Finding a permanent doctor is the hardest part."

"How are you staffing it now?" asked Colin.

"During the summer, I have a couple of medical students from Veracruz come and help out for a month or so, and I try and coerce some doctors from the States to give up their vacation time and come help us out now and then. One of our members, Angelina, has one more year of study in nursing, and then she'll be coming on board full time." Ryan grinned. "I keep hoping she'll marry a doctor who will come here with her."

"That'd be an answer to prayer, wouldn't it?"

"It sure would be. We don't have the resources to hire a doctor full time yet, so until the Lord provides for that, we'll continue to rely on a few dedicated doctors, like Maggie, to help out." Maggie listened attentively to the conversation between the two men.

They talk like they've known each other forever.

"It looks like the Lord has really blessed your efforts here, Ryan," said Colin as he looked around the courtyard.

"He really has. I confess I was worried after the earthquake a few years ago, but there was so much help from the community. We were able to rebuild the dining hall and the damaged cabins in a relatively short amount of time, but there's still a great deal more to do. I'm still learning to trust in the Lord, and to wait for His timing."

"Aren't we all," said Colin as he stood up. "I think I'm ready for that tour. How about you, Maggie?"

"Sounds good!"

They spent the next half hour walking throughout the church grounds with Ryan pointing out the recent repairs, and the places for future expansion. As they returned to the courtyard, Maggie turned to the men and said softly, "If you two don't mind, I'd like to go by the cemetery."

Ryan nodded.

Colin looked into her eyes. "Do you want to go alone?"

"No, I'd really like to have you with me, if you don't mind." She slipped her hand into his and pulled him toward her.

"I don't mind at all, love."

The graveyard was just past a slight rise that gave way to a clearing with flowering bushes and a few small trees. Colin felt Maggie's grip tighten on his hand as they walked along a small gravel pathway that wound throughout the few headstones. Finally, they stopped opposite the stone that marked Scott's grave.

Colin noticed a tear trickle down Maggie's cheek, and he resisted the impulse to wipe it away. He stood quietly, holding her hand.

"I wish you could have known him," whispered Maggie.

"Me, too. He must have been quite a guy to capture your heart."

"I miss him."

"I know you do, and there's nothing wrong with that. I suspect you'll miss him for the rest of your life, Maggie."

"I thought this would be the best place to bury him because he loved it here so much. Sometimes I wish he was closer, so I could visit more often, but I know his heart was here, and this is where he should be."

Maggie gripped Colin's hand. Just then, the afternoon rain began hitting the leaves of the Ceiba trees creating a slow pitter-patter that increased in frequency as the minutes passed. Colin made no move to leave. Finally, Maggie turned away from the gravesite and gazed up at him.

"Thank you." She turned to look at Scott's final resting place one more time. "I guess we better get inside."

Colin was grateful that she wanted him with her. As they walked back to the dining hall, he silently prayed for the woman that he now knew he loved.

CHAPTER THIRTEEN

THE NEXT FEW days flew by as Maggie arranged the clinic to be more efficient, and Colin and Ryan worked on repairing some of the pews in the main sanctuary. Several mothers brought their children in for vaccination updates and pediatric check-ups, grateful that Maggie had returned. As word spread, her daily patient load began to increase, and she chose to work nonstop throughout the day, even through the traditional siesta time. By the early evening, she was ready to rest and spend time with Colin.

On the morning of their first official day off, Colin and Maggie sat on the porch of the dining hall. Colin strummed a guitar and sang some of his favorites hymns, while Maggie closed her eyes, listening to the music.

> *Precious memories, how they linger, how they ever flood my soul*
> *In the stillness of the midnight, precious, sacred scenes unfold.*

She smiled as precious memories of days with Scott came to mind. While Colin continued to sing, the images in Maggie's mind began to fade, replaced with those more recent. She allowed her mind to wander to the night she met Colin, to their first dinner, and then to their walks along the Malibu coastline. She sighed and opened her eyes. Turning her head, she allowed her gaze to fall upon Colin and remain there. He had a peaceful, faraway look as he sang soft and low.

> *Amazing grace, how sweet the sound*
> *That saved a wretch like me,*
> *I once was lost, but now am found*
> *Was blind, but now I see*

"Maggie, come quick!"

Her heart raced at the urgency in Ryan's cry, and she jumped up. Colin placed the guitar against the porch railing and rose to stand by Maggie.

"It's Isabella! Her husband says something is wrong with her, and maybe the baby!"

Maggie's mind immediately replayed the last time she had seen the young Mexican woman. *Eight months pregnant. Prenatal exam was within normal limits. What could be wrong?*

Remembering that Isabella was expecting her first child in about four weeks, Maggie could not recall anything being out of the ordinary in the physical exam. The local midwife had been seeing Isabella every month or so as well, and both she and Maggie anticipated a delivery without complications.

Upon reaching the clinic, Maggie entered the examination room. She sent Isabella's husband, Armando, into the outer room to wait with Colin and Ryan.

"Isabella, what's happening?" asked Maggie as she did a quick initial assessment of mental status, skin color, and pupillary reflex. Her vital signs were within normal limits, including her blood pressure.

"Not so good, Doctora. *Me duele mucho*," gasped Isabella, holding her abdomen.

"When did the pain start?"

"Maybe six or seven hours ago," Isabella said through clenched teeth.

Maggie placed her stethoscope on the young woman's abdomen and hoped she'd pick up a fetal heart tone. After moving the head of the scope several times, she relaxed when she finally heard the rapid beating of the unborn baby's heart.

Maggie felt Isabella's abdomen tighten under her stethoscope.

"Isabella, is it hurting you now?"

"*Sí, Doctora*," cried Isabella, nodding.

"Isabella, I think your baby is about to be born."

Her eyes opened wide. "*No, Doctora*, it's too early, *no?*"

Maggie draped the sheet up over Isabella's legs and prepared to check her progress.

"No, it will be fine. You weren't sure about the dates, remember? According to all the information from your last exam, your baby is well within the window of adequate lung development."

"*¿Cómo?*"

Maggie chuckled. "I'm sorry. Everything's fine. Your baby is healthy and ready to be born. There shouldn't be any problems. Umm … *no hay problema*."

Maggie checked Isabella's progress and realized the birth truly was imminent. "Isabella, looks like your baby is in a rush to be born." Maggie turned toward the waiting room. "Ryan!"

Colin poked his head in. "He took Armando outside. I think he wanted to calm him down. Anything I can do?"

"You sure can! Come in here and wash your hands with that soap solution over there. Then hand me a couple of fresh sheets from that cabinet. I'm deputizing you."

"What?"

"I need a nurse and you're it."

"Oh. Alright. What do I do?"

"I need some fresh sheets, and could you pull that tray table over here? Also, turn that heat lamp on and stick a blanket under it to get it warm."

Maggie turned back to Isabella and repositioned her for the delivery. Taking the linens from Colin, she re-draped her patient for delivery, and prepared to receive the newborn.

"Colin, can you hold her hand and say something reassuring in Spanish?" Maggie moved a rolling stool over to facilitate her position for the delivery. Another quick check informed Maggie of the baby's crowning.

"I can see lots of black hair," said Maggie. "Can you tell her to push with the next contraction?"

Colin made eye contact with Isabella. "*Señora, me llamo Colin. Por favor, empuje con mas fuerza en la próxima contracción. La doctora dice que su bebé tiene mucho pelo negro.*"

Isabella smiled through her discomfort. "*Sí Señor Colin, gracias.*" She paused for a brief moment. "*Oh ... me duele.*"

"*Empuje, señora, empuje,*" urged Colin, holding Isabella's hand while she held her breath and pushed.

As the baby's head began to emerge from the birth canal, Maggie quickly felt for the umbilical cord. It was wrapped around the baby's neck.

"Stop!" commanded Maggie. "Tell her not to push!"

"*¡Pare, señora!*" said Colin. Isabella's fingers squeezed around Colin's as he watched Maggie from where he stood. Never wavering, Maggie deftly moved her fingers to free the vital bloodline from mother to child from the strangulating hold it had around the baby's neck.

"Good. The cord's free," Maggie said to herself, relieved. She glanced up at Colin. "She can push on the next one. Let's get this baby out."

Colin smiled at Isabella. "*En la próxima, empuje señora, bueno?*"

She nodded, her eyes locked on to Colin's. Her grip tightened once more around his fingers as another contraction began. Isabella held her breath and bore down.

Colin whispered in her ear, "*Tú puedes hacerlo, Isabella,* you can do it. *Tú puedes hacerlo.*"

Suddenly the loud, lusty cry of a newborn baby filled the air. Maggie quickly suctioned fluid from the baby's mouth and nose, then wrapped it in the warmed receiving blanket.

"You have a son, Isabella," said Maggie as she placed the child in its mother's arms. Isabella began to weep, her face radiant with joy.

"*Tú tienes un hijo, Isabella,*" repeated Colin softly, wiping his own eyes.

"*Gracias, Doctora, y a tí Señor Colin, muchas gracias.*" Maggie finished the delivery process as Colin continued to comfort the new mother.

"You can go get Armando now," said Maggie as she stood up and removed her gloves. "By the way ..."

Colin stopped and turned toward Maggie.

"You make a great nurse!" Colin grinned as he went into the outer room to find the new father.

"*¡Felicidades, Armando! ¡Es un hijo!*" Colin shook the young man's hand robustly. Armando stood and eyed Colin with uncertainty.

Ryan smiled as he offered his praise to the Lord, "Thank you, Father!"

"Isabella?" asked Armando.

"*Está bien.* She's fine. Go on in." Colin gestured toward the delivery area. He remained in the waiting area with Ryan. "That was incredible, Ryan! I have never witnessed anything like it." He shook his head in amazement. "I tell you, everybody ought to witness a baby being born into this world. There'd be no doubt that there's a God."

"You're right about that. Baby's fine?"

"Yes. I guess there was some problem for a bit. At least, I think so. Maggie got pretty commanding for a while, but then she seemed to relax a bit. I still can't believe it. A new life and I got to witness it!" He sat down in a chair and chuckled. "Sure makes the verse about being 'fearfully and wondrously made' so much more meaningful."

Ryan sat beside Colin and nodded. "Psalm 139 says it all, doesn't it? Armando was so worried that the baby was too early, but God's timing is perfect."

Just then, Maggie came out into the waiting room with a wide grin on her face.

"That was wonderful! It is the ultimate experience as an emergency room doctor. Bringing a life into the world … that's indescribable. And you, Colin, you were terrific!" Maggie sat down next to him and patted his hand. "I hereby deem you an honorary nurse."

"Thanks." Colin beamed. "It was pretty cool; the miracle of life!"

"What happened in there?" Ryan asked. "Colin said there was some kind of problem?"

"One of those normal abnormalities. The umbilical cord was wrapped around the baby's neck. If that's not handled right, the oxygen supply could be cut off, and then you have the potential for brain damage or worse," said Maggie, matter-of-fact. "But it was fairly easy to remove it. Baby's fine. Mom's doing well. I couldn't have asked for a better delivery."

"How's that for divine providence," said Ryan.

Maggie smiled and nodded. "I'm with you on that one."

"Me, too," added Colin. "I'm still feeling the effects of the rush. So much for siesta time."

"I'm going back in to check on my patients," said Maggie. She stood and stretched, then headed to Isabella's room. "You two go celebrate and I'll catch up with you in a little while."

"I think we all deserve some rest," said Ryan. "I'll meet you later for dinner." He patted Colin on the back and added, "What a glorious day this has been!" He left, whistling *Jesus Loves Me*.

After he watched Maggie disappear into the clinic treatment area, Colin turned his eyes upward. "This has been quite a ride, Lord. I could do this kind of work for a long time."

He stood up and headed toward the porch of the dining hall, but stopped midway between the hall and the sanctuary. He surveyed the church, the dining hall, and the clinic. "I could do this, couldn't I, Lord?" His previously random thoughts began to come together in his mind. "Is this what Your plan is for me? It would be awesome, Lord. I've been praying for direction for a long time. Is this really it?" He turned quickly and sprinted toward the pastor's office.

"Ryan! Ryan!" He called out, bursting through the office door.

Ryan looked up at him in alarm. "Is something wrong?" he asked, quickly rising from his chair.

"No, not at all." Colin grabbed a nearby chair and plunked down on it. "Listen, I've been praying for quite a while about how I can be of greater service to God, and I think I've got it!"

Ryan sat down, his face puzzled.

Colin continued without stopping to take a breath. "This is such a wonderful thing that God has led you to do here. I mean, the possibilities are endless. The only thing hindering you is money, right? So, what if I back you? You need funds to finish building the assembly hall. I've got the means to provide it!

"I'd be strictly a silent partner. However, I'd love to come here and help out now and then, but you'd still be in charge one hundred percent."

Ryan's eyes grew wide. "Are you serious about this?"

"Absolutely." Colin rested his forearms on Ryan's desk. "We could even hire a doctor or nurse, or whatever, until the ones you've got lined up finish school and come back. Your clinic could be up and running full time right away!"

"I don't know what to say." Ryan sat back in his chair. "I've been praying that God would provide, and He always has, but I never expected this."

"I'd be honored if you'd let me be a part of God's work here. I don't know too much about the business end of this kind of stuff, but my accountant can set everything up for you, and then you'll pretty much be on your own."

Ryan stood up. "Give me a moment." He took a few steps away from the table, toward a window facing the courtyard.

Colin watched him, knowing that Ryan was praying.

Lord, this feels so right. Please give us both peace about this. If it's not Your will, please close the door right now. Don't let Ryan agree with me unless it is Your will, and then, let us be in complete agreement. Colin continued to pray in silence.

For a short while, the only sound in the office was the whirring of the overhead fan. Then Ryan turned around to face Colin.

"I never thought God would answer my prayers this way," admitted Ryan as he extended his hand to Colin. "I'd love to have you working with us. I can't begin to tell you what this means, not just to me, but also to the people here. Having the clinic up and running on a permanent basis … it's a doorway to establishing relationships that will allow us to share the gospel with so many folks in this community."

Colin heartily shook Ryan's hand. "I've got to admit, this wasn't really the reason why I came down here, but God has a way of doing the unexpected, doesn't He?"

"Yes, He certainly does." Ryan looked directly at Colin. "So, why did you come?"

Colin took a deep breath.

How am I supposed to answer that?

"I, uh, well, Maggie asked, and I— "

Ryan nodded knowingly. "You like her?"

Colin felt very self-conscious, but decided that honesty was needed. "Yes, I like her very much, but … until she's saved, I just can't pursue a deeper relationship. But it's really hard, Ryan." He took a deep breath. "And then there's Scott."

"I understand," said Ryan. "I believe that the Lord will work in her heart in His time. It's been hard on her since Scott died. She couldn't understand how God could take him away from her. It was a very difficult time for her, and me, for that matter, but I had the Scriptures for comfort. All she had was her work. It was almost an entire year before she came back here, and that was only after I had asked many, many times.

"On the morning that Scott died, Maggie had come to me and told me that she wanted to talk about my faith. I was so hopeful, and then the quake happened. We never did have the chance to talk after that, and she's never brought it up since. I didn't understand how God could allow that opportunity to slip away, but I knew I had to trust Him."

At that moment, Maggie knocked on the open door of the office.

"Hi guys, what's going on?"

Ryan looked at Colin, then Maggie. "The Lord has just answered a prayer." He quickly recounted Colin's offer to her.

Maggie's mouth dropped. She glanced at Colin, then Ryan, then back to Colin.

"What? You can't be serious!" Her fiery gaze focused on Colin's surprised look. "How could you? You can't just walk in here and take over!" Her hands formed fists at her side. "I don't believe this!"

Colin blinked as Maggie stormed off. "What just happened?"

"I don't know, but something's not right."

"That's an understatement. I thought she'd be happy about this. I'd better go talk with her."

Ryan stood and put his hand on Colin's shoulder. "Let me go."

Reluctantly, Colin nodded.

Lord, what happened? What did I do wrong? This is Your plan, right? But Maggie, she's furious with me. His heart felt heavy, and he continued to pray, trying desperately to believe that no matter how things appeared, God was still in control, and all things would be made good in His time.

"Maggie?" called Ryan as he knocked on her door. When she didn't answer, he knocked again. "Maggie, can I come in?"

No answer came, so Ryan opened the door slowly.

"Maggie? I'm coming in."

He entered her cabin and found her sitting on the edge of her bed. She sat with her hands clasped in her lap, and made no move to rise or greet him.

"Maggie, what's wrong?" He saw the tracks of tears on her face.

"He can't do this, Ryan! This is not his ministry. It's yours and Scott's. It's not right."

"He believes this is what God wants him to do, Maggie. Colin is just trying to serve God."

"He sings for God."

"He wants to do more. He believes that God led him here to help us. To get the clinic up and running permanently. That is something we both want, right?"

Maggie pressed her lips together, closed her eyes, and sighed. "Of course, I want the clinic to be staffed full time, and I'm glad he can help do that."

"You have a strange way of showing that, Maggie."

"I guess I'm not really sure how I feel about it. I mean, the clinic part is good, but this isn't his work—it's not his ministry. You and Scott built this place from nothing. This is *your* work and Scott's."

Ryan rested a hand on his sister-in-law's shoulder and silently asked God to help him choose the right words to say to her. "It's not *my* work, or Scott's, for that matter, Maggie. It's God's work. I'm a servant, just like Scott was, and just like Colin is. We're doing *God's* work here." A thin smile crept across his lips; he hoped Maggie could understand what he was saying.

"Running a facility like this takes all kinds of servants. Some are builders, some cook, others keep the records. Some ..." he looked directly at her, "... come periodically and help with the medical needs. Me, I'm only a teacher and a pastor. I'm a servant just like everyone else, and none of us can do it alone. Some people, like Colin, serve in a totally different capacity. They help with the financing."

"So, you're perfectly OK with this?"

"Not only am I OK with it, I believe that Scott would be fine with it, too. I know he's no longer with us, Maggie, but God's work remains, and that's what has to continue, no matter who's involved. Scott would definitely want that.

"If he were here, my brother would welcome Colin's help with open arms, and I believe he'd want you to do the same. This place …" Ryan waved his hand around in a circle, "… it's not a memorial to my brother, Maggie. It's a vibrant ministry for Christ." He let out a deep breath and walked to the door, then turned back to his sister-in-law. "I love you, Maggie. Nothing will ever change that. I know it's hard for you. It's hard for me. I miss him, too, but I know he would want us to go on, and more than that, I know God wants us to go on. Colin's help, well, it's just another answer to a prayer that will keep this work alive. That's what I want, that's what Scott would want, and I believe, that's what you want deep inside."

Tears began to fall as Maggie stood up and walked over to her brother-in-law.

"Why is this so hard for me?" She fell into his arms and cried on his shoulder.

"Because you loved my brother, Maggie. And maybe you're afraid that Colin is going to replace him. But he won't, not here, and not in your heart. Hold on to your memories, Maggie, but don't be afraid to live." Ryan held her at arm's length, his two hands on her shoulders. "I know you'll get through this; God will give you the strength." He hugged her once more. "I'll be praying for you, and I'm here for you if you need me."

She sniffed and nodded, watching him go and reflecting on his words.

Knowing the sanctuary would be empty, Colin plodded to the small wooden structure after he saw Ryan enter Maggie's cabin. Momentarily standing in the aisle, he glanced around the church, and then walked up to the piano. He ran one finger over the keys and sat down on the bench as the notes faded.

"Lord, I don't know what happened, and even worse, I don't know how to make it right. I thought this was Your will," Colin said, his voice heavy. "And I thought Maggie would be happy about it."

He lifted his head up slowly, and sat for a few more minutes. Then he placed his hands over the keys, and started to play. His music filled the sanctuary, and his despair began to fade. He closed his eyes and let the music blanket him in a cloud of serenity. It wasn't until the setting sun's light began to filter into the sanctuary that he realized he was not alone. Finishing the piece he was playing, he glanced toward the entrance of the church and saw Maggie's silhouette in the doorway. He stood up quickly and walked toward the back of the church.

Maggie marched steadily toward Colin. When she reached him, he started to speak, but Maggie put her hand up to silence him.

She took a deep breath. "I am so sorry."

When Colin started to speak again, she put a finger to his lips.

"I don't really know what to say to make this right, but I am sorry. I … I shouldn't have walked away. Please forgive me. I acted in haste; I didn't think; I'm an idiot."

"You're not an idiot, Maggie. Far from it. Just tell me, what did I do?" He hesitated to ask what he thought was obvious. "Is it the money?"

Maggie shook her head slightly before answering. "No. Not really. I think … this place is all I have left of Scott, and I guess I'm afraid if you get involved, I'll lose part of him. I don't know how to deal with that. This place is so special to me, because it was special to Scott, and I feel so close to him when I'm here. I don't want to lose that feeling. I still love him, Colin. This is the place where I feel most connected to him."

What am I supposed to say to that? I can't compete with a memory.

Maggie turned her eyes to the cross over the pulpit. "Ryan came to my cabin to talk to me after I left you in his office. He tried to explain everything to me. I've been thinking … a lot about what he said. I don't even know where to start."

Colin brushed a tear from her cheek and motioned for her to sit on the pew beside him.

Maggie looked at him through her moist eyes, and her voice shook. "I am so sorry. Can you ever forgive me?"

His heart almost broke; the agony he felt for her was almost unbearable.

Could I just hold you, Maggie? Could I just tell you that I love you? Kiss away all the hurt and confusion? Oh God, I don't know how much more of this I can take. He took her hand in his.

Maggie spoke so quietly that Colin could barely hear her. "Ryan talked about being a servant of God's and that's the reason you're giving the money. He said that's what you and he are … servants. That's why you want to help. I thought … I thought maybe you were trying to replace Scott."

Colin brushed a wisp of hair away from her eye. "I'm just a singer, Maggie. I don't really get to serve God in the same way Ryan or Jesse do. I sing and hope someone, somewhere hears my music, and God uses it to minister to their heart, but I don't really have the opportunity to ... to ... be a part of His work firsthand. But here, there's so much that I can do personally. Maybe that's selfish of me to want to be involved like that, but God has blessed me so much in my career ... especially financially, and I've been praying for a way to give back to Him. This ministry can bring the gospel to many people in this area, but Ryan needs the funds to be able to do that. All I'm hoping to do is provide those funds, not erase the memory of Scott ... here or in your heart."

They sat together in silence for quite a while until Maggie spoke.

"I think I understand that, well, partly. I know you're trying to do what God wants you to do, but I don't know how you know this is it. Why not an orphanage or even Jesse's church? How do you know it's here? I guess I just don't understand how your faith works." Maggie shook her head. "I know it's so different from mine. Same God, same Bible, but something's very different. I've watched you, for a long time, and I've seen it. There really is something very different about you and your relationship with God ... same as Scott."

She stared down at their hands and continued in a whisper. "You seem so, so personal with God. Like He's right here with you. Like you *know* Him. I know we talked a little about this before, but I guess I still don't really understand it."

Colin placed a finger under Maggie's chin and turned her face up to his eyes. Her brow was furrowed, her lips tightly drawn. *Lord, please help me say the right words. I need Your Holy Spirit now more than ever, Lord. Please, help me lead her to Christ.*

He drew a breath and began. "You're right, Maggie; God is right here with me ... with us. My faith is based upon the relationship I have with Christ. I got saved, meaning I accepted Jesus into my life, when I was a little boy. I went to church, learned my Sunday school lessons, memorized verses, all that stuff, but it wasn't until my mid-twenties when I understood that God wanted a personal relationship with me. The only way I could have that was to surrender my life to Him, to make Him first in my life. It wasn't enough to know that Christ died on the cross for me; I needed to make Him the Savior of my life. So, I did that. I prayed and asked Him to forgive me, all my sins, my years of resistance, my desire to do things my way … everything."

"That seems rather simplistic."

Colin felt a new boldness. "That part is, Maggie. God knows there is nothing that you or I could do that would merit His mercy and forgiveness, so He sacrificed His own Son to pay the price for our sins. All we have to do is ask Him for that forgiveness, and He gives it, unconditionally. The hard part is serving Him afterwards. It's a daily struggle for all Christians, but it's also how we grow in our faith."

"And that's it? Then you have this … this relationship with God?" She looked directly into his blue eyes.

"Yes, but He'll never force that relationship upon you. Jesus just waits. He'll wait as long as it takes because that's why He went to the cross. To have a relationship with you. To be your personal Savior."

Maggie shifted in the pew. "Let me see if I understand this correctly. You're saying all I need to do is ask Jesus to forgive me, and I get to have this same relationship with God that you have?" She tilted her head.

"Yes, if you sincerely want His forgiveness and you're willing for Him to be your Lord and Savior, that's all you need to do. There is no magic formula. There's nothing you can do to earn it. It's God's gift to us through His Son. Only Jesus saves us from our sins and makes a relationship with God possible."

"So all the church going didn't amount to anything?"

"On the contrary. All the church going was like laying a foundation. You gained a lot of head knowledge about God. You were able to see people whose lives centered on God, like Scott. You saw Christianity in action, and even participated in some of it. Like here at Santa Molina. You're part of Ryan's ministry. You just need to take that final step.

Colin sat back against the pew and gazed steadily at Maggie. "It's like you've been on a long journey, and now you've finally reached your home, but you're not really home until you open the door and walk in. You've learned a lot about God, but until you give Him your heart, you're not really home."

She sat without speaking.

"Maggie, maybe you should be talking to Ryan about this. This is more his specialty."

She shook her head. "No, I just need to think about this. I think I'll just go back to my cabin and think about all of this. You will be praying for me, won't you?"

"I have been, and I will be," said Colin as a smile touched his lips. "Can I pray for you right now?"

"Now?"

Colin nodded and bowed his head. Maggie lowered her head and closed her eyes. He reached for her hands, and held them firmly.

"Father, Maggie is searching for answers that only You can provide. Please help her find those answers, Lord, and reveal Yourself to her just like you did to me." His voice slightly faltered. "Lord, I know that there is no way to perfect peace and contentment without Jesus. In Your infinite mercy and grace, and through the power of Your Holy Spirit, please open her eyes to who You are, and how much You love her. Help her understand that the way to You is through the cross of Christ. May Your will be done in her life, and in Your time. I love You, Lord, and I ask these things in the name of Your Son, Jesus. Amen."

"Thank you," she whispered as she squeezed his hands.

"You're welcome, Maggie. Let me know if there's anything I can do to help you." He stood and helped her to her feet.

Maggie gave him a quick hug. "You already have."

Colin watched her leave the sanctuary, then he walked up to the front pew. He stood for a moment gazing up at the large wooden cross on the wall behind the pulpit area. Turning, he knelt before the first pew, folded his hands and bowed his head.

CHAPTER FOURTEEN

MAGGIE ENTERED HER cabin, walked to the small closet, and withdrew her suitcase. Laying it on her bed, she opened it and pulled out a very familiar Bible. Sitting on the edge of the bed, she ran her fingers over the black leather cover, stopping on the name of her husband inscribed in gold lettering near the bottom. Setting the Bible down on the bedside table, she put the suitcase back in the closet, then made herself comfortable on the bed before opening the book.

Not knowing where to turn, Maggie decided it was time to try a prayer of her own.

"God, if You're listening to me, I'm asking for some help. I've always been pretty independent, and I've done very well in my life without being overly religious, but I do know that something's not altogether right between us. I'm not one to just accept something because someone's told me, so I would appreciate it if You could help me find something in this Bible that will help me understand it all." She hesitated, then ended with a simple "Amen."

She began to thumb through Scott's Bible, recognizing the familiar notations he often made in the margins. She decided that those notes would be a good place to start, so she began to read them and the verses to which they referred. To understand some, she was forced to read entire chapters, but others still remained beyond her comprehension.

Since many of the verses in the book of John were highlighted, Maggie decided to read the entire book. Drawn to the story between Nicodemus and Jesus, she reread chapter three.

For God so loved the world that He gave His only begotten Son, that whosoever believeth in Him should not perish, but have everlasting life. For God sent not his Son into the world to condemn the world; but that the world through Him might be saved.

"But I do believe that, God," maintained Maggie. She thought back on one of her conversations with Colin. It wasn't enough to just believe, he had said. She needed to make a conscious choice to have the relationship. "I don't get it, Lord. I believe in You. I really do. What else do I have to do to have the same thing everyone else has?"

It's like a vaccine.

Maggie stopped abruptly.

A vaccine? How in the world is a vaccine related to my belief in God?

She closed the Bible in her lap, and focused her thinking on vaccines and their role in medicine. *Vaccines were manufactured to save lives. Millions of people died from polio, diphtheria, measles, and many other diseases prior to the discovery of live-saving vaccines. Today, due to vaccines, these diseases are no longer the threat they once were. However, some people still refuse to use them.*

"Is that it? Is it that simple? OK, God. Let's see if I have this right. It's sort of like a vaccine. I can believe the vaccine will eradicate a disease, but unless I actually choose to use it, my belief in it is useless." Maggie leaned up straight against the wall behind her bed. "So that makes Christ the vaccine and sin the disease. Without accepting Christ and allowing Him to save me, the sin is still there, and it will ultimately destroy me."

She continued to read the rest of the book of John, but her mind kept returning to John 3:16 and 17 as she struggled to grasp the enormity of the love of God for her and the simplicity of His plan for salvation.

Unsure of where to go after she finished the chapter, she thumbed through the Bible until she reached the inside back cover. Scott had written the words, 'The Roman's Road to Salvation' and under them, he had written several verses. She didn't know if these verses would help her understanding, but she believed if Scott had written them down, they had to be important. She quickly located the book of Romans and flipped the pages until she found chapter three, verse twenty-three, the first verse in Scott's list.

For all have sinned and come short of the glory of God.

As she pondered the verse, she saw that next to it, Scott had written the location of the second verse in "the Road." Each subsequent verse she turned to had the next verse penciled in, so she read all of the verses in Scott's list.

Maggie read the last reference, Romans 10:9-10, silently, then again aloud.

"That if thou shalt confess with thy mouth the Lord Jesus, and shalt believe in thine heart that God hath raised Him from the dead, thou shalt be saved. For with the heart man believeth unto righteousness; and with the mouth confession is made unto salvation."

Scott had drawn an arrow from verse ten to verse thirteen. Again, Maggie read out loud.

"For whosoever shall call upon the name of the Lord shall be saved."

The last notation directed her to the second chapter of Ephesians, verses eight and nine.

For by grace are ye saved through faith; and that not of yourselves: it is the gift of God: Not of works, lest any man should boast.

She set the Bible down on the bed as her mind continually returned to the image of a vaccine sitting useless on a counter, ready to save a life, yet no one choosing to use it. She thought of the children in Santa Molina who no longer had to worry about life-threatening diseases due to the vaccines delivered to them. She closed the Bible, and once again Maggie talked, plain and simply to God.

"God, I don't know what to do. Can you please help me? There's so much I don't understand. And this ..." She picked up the Bible and stared at the cover, "... this has so much in it. How can I ever find what I need?" She tossed the book back on the bed and it fell open. She stared at it for a moment.

"No." She shook her head. "That only happens in the movies." She sat still a little longer, staring at the open Bible.

"Is this some kind of test?" She took a deep breath, picked up the Bible, and began to read where it had opened.

Near the center of the page were two verses that Scott had highlighted. As she read them, Maggie sucked in her breath.

Trust in the Lord with all thine heart; and lean not unto thine own understanding. In all thy ways acknowledge Him, and He shall direct thy paths.

"Are you trying to scare me?" Maggie asked aloud, wondering if God really heard her, but knowing deep within her heart that He did.

She sat perfectly still, her tears threatening to spill over her eyelids. There was a battle waging deep within her soul, and she knew it was time to make a decision that would change her life forever, one way or another. Either she would accept all that God had to offer her, or she would reject Him and continue to live as she had.

Despite her efforts, tears began to fall, and her body trembled. Clutching the Bible to her chest, she cried until she could cry no more. The anguish she felt from her hesitance to accept God's gift of salvation tore at her soul, and she wrestled with the resistance within her own reluctant heart.

During the darkest hours of the night, her searching came to an end. Maggie Devereaux quietly bowed her head before the Lord, sought His forgiveness, and surrendered her life to the One who so willingly sacrificed His own on an old rugged cross for her.

The early morning hours were resplendent as the sun peeked over the horizon, spilling its hues of pink, blue, and purple on an awakening world. Finishing his morning devotions, Colin emerged from his cabin into the courtyard. Except for a tiny sparrow perched on a wooden bench, it was devoid of any activity. The cheery bird's song filled the morning air, and Colin reflected on one of his favorite hymns.

Let not your heart be troubled, His tender word I hear,
And resting on His goodness, I lose my doubts and fear;
Though by the path He leads me, But one step I may see:
His eye is on the sparrow, and I know He watches me.

Colin had been up for most of the night, praying for the woman he had grown to love. Now, he desperately wanted to go to her, but he felt led to wait, so he sat down on the same bench the songbird just left.

A few minutes later, he saw Maggie appear from her cabin. She ran over to him and grabbed both of his hands.

"Guess what?" Her eyes sparkled. "I surrendered my life to God!"

Colin stared at her, his eyes wide. Before he could speak, Maggie excitedly continued.

"I did it! I told Him I was His, all of me ... everything! I asked Him to save me, and He did!" Her tears flowed freely down her cheeks, but her eyes never left Colin's. "I am now officially a Christian, and I'm so grateful for you never giving up on me." Her voice broke. "I ... I can't thank you enough."

Colin pulled her to him and held her against him. "Praise God!" he whispered huskily as he hugged her tightly. He buried his face in her hair as his tears spilled over. "I cannot tell you how happy I am for you, Maggie!"

"Did you keep your promise?" asked Maggie pulling away from him. She gazed into his warm, blue eyes.

"Yes, I did, love. I prayed all night."

"Thank you!" She kissed him on the cheek. "I can't wait to tell Ryan. Let's go find him!"

They hurried to the dining room, and as they entered, Ryan glanced up from his table. He closed his Bible and rose to greet them, halfway to his table.

"Welcome home, sister!" said Ryan as he embraced Maggie. "And I mean that in a spiritual sense."

Maggie's mouth fell open. "How did you know?"

Ryan grinned. "It's one of those things that is tough to hide. You're wearing your joy on your face. Getting saved does that to people."

Maggie waved her hands around. "It was just like med school—a marathon of studying all through the night. I read, thought, paced, read some more, thought some more, and when I felt like I was going nowhere, I gave up. But that's when … it was like … like God was talking to me. Not some mystical voice or anything like that, but this … this still, small voice inside of me. Does that make any sense?"

Ryan and Colin smiled at each other, then said, "Yes!"

Colin was overcome with joy. After pouring fresh coffee for all, he sipped from his cup as Maggie shared her story of salvation.

CHAPTER FIFTEEN

I T'S GOOD TO have you back, Maggie," said Valerie as they each enjoyed a cup of coffee during a lull in the emergency room.

"It's good to be back. I missed you and Will." She signed off on a patient's chart and placed it in a pile designated for discharged patients.

"How's Colin doing?"

"Great. We're having dinner tomorrow." She laughed, then said, "You should've seen him helping me deliver a baby in Santa Molina. He was awesome!"

"I would've loved to have been there. Sounds like you two had a wonderful time."

"We did. In so many ways. I have so much I want to tell you."

Valerie opened her mouth to speak when a loud masculine voice came from one of the treatment rooms.

"Get me out of here! I want to go home!"

"I'll go." Maggie rushed out of the lounge and headed to the room from where the voice emanated. She glanced at the chart to read the patient's name as she moved to the bedside. Placing a hand on the old, wrinkled hand of Neil Russell, she spoke in a low, soft voice.

"What's wrong, Mr. Russell?"

The elderly man scowled. "They don't know what they're doing in here. That doctor was young enough to be my grandson. He can't be no decent doctor. I want to go home. Let me go home!"

Maggie pulled up a chair and sat beside the bed.

"What did he tell you?"

"Something about my heart. But my ticker's just fine! He don't know a thing he's talking about. Said he was going to go talk to my daughter. She don't need to be here. Got three young'uns of her own. She didn't need to drag me down here. I'm fine!"

Maggie grinned. "Three grandchildren? Wow! Can you tell me about them?"

"Three of the best grand young'uns you ever saw." Neil chuckled. "Peter, he's the oldest; he's almost ten years old. Loves to fish. We go up to the mountains and catch trout. The other two are girls. Stella and Dawn. They're seven and six. Cute as a bug's ear. Not into fishing, not like Peter, but they love to go camping with me and their momma and daddy. I taught 'em how to build a campfire last summer." Neil's eyes grew moist. "We're going again, and I aim to teach them girls how to catch trout."

Maggie leaned forward. "I'll bet they love going with you."

"They sure do, Miss. You got kids?"

"No, not yet."

"Peter, he's the spittin' image of his momma," Neil said, gazing at the ceiling. "His daddy's an accountant. Don't know too much about camping, but sure does give it his all when we go."

Maggie picked up the elderly man's chart from the bedside table, perused the lab results, and glanced up at the muted cardiac monitor. The rhythm and rate seemed relatively normal, but the electrocardiogram indicated atrial fibrillation. Knowing this could be treated with medications, Maggie assumed Mr. Russell would be admitted for observation and treatment, then released with a cardiology referral for follow-up.

"Mr. Russell, don't you think Peter and the girls would like their grandfather to be as healthy as possible to go on these camping trips?" she asked gazing steadily into the grey-blue eyes of the patient.

"… Hmmm … I s'pose so. I know where you're going with this, Missy."

Maggie chuckled. "I'm sure you do, sir, but once we make sure there's nothing wrong with your heart, we can send you home, and your daughter won't have to worry so much about you. You'll be ready for those fishing trips, and everyone, especially those grandchildren of yours, will be happy. Hopefully, it won't be more than a day or so in the hospital. You know, we've always got to run tests, and those do take some time."

"Too many ridiculous tests. I don't need them," he grumbled.

"Maybe you don't, Mr. Russell, but it would sure make our jobs a bit easier if we knew exactly what we were dealing with. How about it? Two days, three tops, and then you're out. Please? It'd go awfully good for me if I could tell my boss you consented to these tests."

Neil grinned at Maggie and patted her hand. "You are one sweet nurse, Missy. OK, it's a deal, but if'n I have to stay here longer'n three days, I'm going raise quite a ruckus, and—"

"Agreed," said Maggie as she stood up. "I'll go make sure your daughter's informed of our discussion and your decision." She started to leave when Neil called out.

"If all the nurses in this hospital are like you, maybe it won't be so bad."

Maggie smiled. "I hope it won't be. You get some rest, and someone will be back here in a bit."

He gave her a thumbs-up as she stepped to the other side of the curtain. Standing there were Valerie, a security officer, Dr. Markham, Neil's admitting doctor, and the patient's daughter.

"Bravo, *Nurse* Devereaux," whispered Valerie. "You did a great job."

"Yes, you did," concurred Dr. Markham. "I presume it's safe to go in, *Nurse?*" He grinned as he stepped toward the curtain and motioned for Neil's daughter to follow him.

"Thank you," the daughter mouthed.

Maggie nodded and walked with Valerie to the nurse's station.

"Impressive! I was right! You do make one great nurse!" Valerie's eyes twinkled as she spoke.

"I've got a fabulous role model," said Maggie with a soft elbow nudge to Valerie's arm.

Ever since Maggie's return from her last trip to Santa Molina, Valerie had sensed some sort of change in her, but she was unable to pinpoint it. They hadn't had a chance to talk, but whatever had happened, Valerie deduced that it was behind the subtle difference in Maggie. She wanted to believe it had something to do with a growing relationship between her sister-in-law and one very handsome singer, but she would address that later. Now her attention turned to a young mother standing at the nurses' station with a baby in her arms.

"May I help you?"

She can't be older than seventeen or eighteen.

"I think my baby's got measles," said the mother, clutching her daughter. "She's had a fever for two days, and this awful rash."

"Let's move you into a room, and see what's going on, OK?" She led the mother to the examination area, took a brief history, and checked the six-week-old baby's vital signs.

"Well, she does have a slight temperature. Have you given her anything?" asked Valerie, making notes as Francie, the baby's mother, responded.

"No, just let her sleep in her diapers. No shirt, but then she got this rash, and, well, I got scared. So I came in."

"Who's her pediatrician?"

"We ... Molly doesn't have one."

"When was the last time she saw a doctor?"

Receiving no answer, Valerie asked, "Has any doctor seen her since she was born?"

"No, no. I don't have insurance." Panic filled Francie's eyes. "She won't die, will she?"

Valerie took a deep breath. "We're going to do everything to help her. You wait right here. I'll be right back."

Valerie found Maggie writing a discharge summary at the nurses' station.

"When you're done, can you see a possible case of measles? Teen mom, no postnatal care for the baby, who's six-weeks-old."

"Measles? Whose on call for peds? Is the baby in isolation?"

Valerie nodded, then scowled, "McEverett, but he hasn't answered his page yet."

Maggie frowned. "Does he ever? Sure, let me finish this, and I'll go right in."

"Thanks, you're the best."

I can always count on you, Mags. It doesn't matter what's going on, you're always there to help. I wish the other docs were like you.

A few minutes later, Maggie was talking with Francie about her baby. She did a thorough exam, making several notes on the chart while listening to the mother's story.

"The good news is it's not measles," said Maggie. "It's just a viral illness that needs to run its course. However, there are a few other concerns I have."

The teen's eyes widened.

Maggie pulled up a chair beside Francie and took her hands. "Molly's going to be fine, but she needs to be seen regularly by a pediatrician."

Francie bit her bottom lip and averted her eyes from Maggie's. "I don't have insurance. I'm a waitress. I work nights, and my mom watches her for me. I'm trying to save some money, but that's supposed to be for school."

"When you were in the hospital, did anyone from social services talk to you about getting some assistance?" Maggie released Francie's hands and made a few additional notes on the baby's chart. She looked up when the mother didn't answer.

"I … she wasn't born … in a hospital. Molly was born at home."

Maggie's mouth dropped open. "You've never seen a doctor?"

"No, ma'am." Silent tears fell down the teen's cheeks.

Maggie sighed and regained her composure. She tried to think of a way to reassure the young mother, yet impress upon her the need for medical follow-up for both her and her daughter. She took hold of the mother's hands again. "Francie, it looks like we need to get you hooked up with some help, for you and your daughter. Will that be OK?"

"They won't take my baby away, will they?"

Maggie reached out and touched her shoulder. "Absolutely not. You've been doing a good job with Molly, and you've got your mom's help. Social services will get you and Molly the assistance you need. I'll write the orders for something to help Molly through this sickness, then we'll get someone down here to talk to you about getting that help. Does that sound OK to you?"

Francie held Molly close to her. "Yes, yes, Doctor." A small smile crossed her lips. "That would be wonderful. I really do want to be a good mother. Whatever I need to do, I'll do. Thank you so much."

"You're welcome, Francie. I'll come by in a bit and see how you're doing," said Maggie as she stood up.

Lord, she's got a rough road ahead of her. She's going to need all the help You can give her. Maggie stopped for a moment in the doorway. *Did I just pray for that girl? Wow! That's the first time I've done that.*

Walking over to the nurse's station, she asked the clerk if she had heard from Dr. McEverett.

"Not yet, Dr. Devereaux."

Maggie frowned, then handed the completed chart to the clerk. "Can you get a social worker down here for this patient? And page McEverett again, please."

CHAPTER SIXTEEN

THIS IS SO nice, Colin," said Maggie as she walked out onto his deck. The table was set with two place settings, a spring bouquet in the center, and a platter of assorted cheeses and crackers. Holding a glass of raspberry tea, she leaned on the railing and glanced out toward the ocean. "What a lovely sunset this is going to be," she commented, sipping her tea.

Colin slid up next to Maggie. "I hope so. Are you hungry?"

"Yes, I am. I've been looking forward to your cooking all day."

"Really? Well, in that case, I'll get started. How do you like your steak?" He hurried into the house and returned with two seasoned rib eyes.

"Medium rare would be nice." She turned toward him and leaned against the rail. "Is there anything I can help you with? Or should I just stand here munching on the cheese and crackers?"

"I think everything is pretty much ready. You can just stand there and keep me company while I slave over this hot grill!"

"My pleasure." She popped another cracker into her mouth. "I talked to Ryan this morning. He was so excited about this new doctor coming next week."

"Really? That's great! Where's he coming from?" Colin closed the lid on the grill.

"I'm not sure. Ryan said that he's actually been there before on a short mission trip. I guess he just called Ryan out of the blue and asked if he could talk with him about coming down for an extended stay. Ryan said they talked for a while on the phone, and then he invited this guy to come for a visit. So, he's coming next week."

Colin leaned on the railing next to Maggie and took a sip of soda. "It always amazes me to see how fast God moves His plans into action."

"Especially when you get out of the way and let Him work," Maggie quipped, smiling. "I have so much to learn, Colin."

"We all do, love. We are a work in progress." Colin eyed the sky. "Not to be completed until Jesus returns for us. I'll be right back."

Maggie watched him leave. *This is perfect. A beautiful sunset on the beach and a wonderful guy to be with.*

She stopped mid-thought, surprised at where her thoughts were going. Her heart pounded, and she didn't understand why she suddenly felt uncomfortable thinking about Colin. She closed her eyes and willed herself to think about something else, anything else, but all she could see in her mind was Colin. She was relieved when he returned with salads, corn on the cob, and asparagus spears.

"Looks like quite a feast!" Maggie smiled, quickly composing herself.

"Well, I hope it tastes as good as it looks. Come, sit down before things get cold."

After Colin said grace, they both enjoyed the meal and soon the thoughts that had troubled her earlier vanished. They made light conversation as the last rays of the golden sun sank below the horizon, transforming the blue western sky into a multicolored collage of yellows, pinks, and gold.

Maggie stood up and reached for Colin's hand. "Let's go down to the beach!" She pulled him toward her.

"I love this so much," said Maggie as they sauntered along the water's edge. "It's so beautiful and so peaceful." The ocean breeze whipped her hair around her face. Colin reached forward to brush it from her eyes, and for a moment, their eyes locked and neither of them moved.

Colin tilted her face up toward him, gazed into her eyes, and kissed her.

Maggie yielded herself to his embrace and returned his kiss without reservation.

Suddenly, she pushed herself away from him.

"No, I can't!"

Colin stepped back quickly and drew his hands back as if he had touched a hot surface.

"Maggie, I'm sorry—"

She turned away from him, her hand over her mouth.

"I have to go." She turned toward his house.

Colin grabbed her by the arm. "Wait, Maggie, please. I'm sorry. Let me explain."

Maggie yielded to his hold, but did not turn to face him.

"I'm sorry. I shouldn't have done that. Please forgive me." His voice was barely a whisper. "Please don't go."

Maggie's heart begged her to stay, but her head knew if she did, that she would be unable to resist Colin any longer. Her thoughts fought for her attention. Visions of her courtship with Scott, their wedding and honeymoon, were interlaced with images of Colin—their meeting in the emergency room, their walks on the beach, the trip to Santa Molina, and now, the kiss.

Maggie gazed up at Colin through eyes brimming with tears. She spoke haltingly, "I can't love you; it's … it's impossible."

"Impossible, why?"

"I … I … can't forget Scott."

"Maggie, I'm not asking you to forget Scott. I'm asking you if there's room in your heart for two." He grasped both of her hands.

Maggie shook her head. "No … I thought we were friends. You said we'd just be friends." She turned and walked toward the patio, away from him.

He quickly followed her to the sliding door. She was trembling as she reached to open it.

"Please, Maggie, I'm sorry."

She made no move to open the door, but didn't turn to face him. "I think I should probably go home."

"Are you sure? You're upset. Maybe you shouldn't be driving just yet. I could take you home. I could get your car to you tomorrow."

"No, no, I'll be fine. Really I will be." She reached for her jacket. "Thank you for dinner."

Colin watched her close the front door behind her, then sat on the arm of the sofa. He ran his fingers through his hair, then dropped to his knees. He bowed his head and prayed to the only One who could ease the pain in his broken heart.

The next three days were extremely hectic in the emergency room. Although she missed hearing Colin's voice and desperately wanted to talk with him about the other night, Maggie was unable to find time to call him.

On the afternoon of the third day of nonstop ER madness, Colin entered the emergency room, holding a paper bag. The waiting area was about half full. Amidst the coughing and crying, he made his way to the nurses' station. Valerie came out of a nearby storage room. Her arms were filled with intravenous supplies that threatened to topple to the floor.

"Need a hand?" Colin asked, smiling, as he took three large bags of saline from the top of her load.

"Hey, stranger! Thanks. Looking for Maggie?" Valerie led Colin to a supply cart.

"Yeah. Is she around?"

"She should be out in just a few minutes. I think she's discharging a patient."

"Thanks. Mind if I wait over there?" He indicated a space near the nurses' station, but out of the waiting room area.

"Not at all. It's been a zoo around here these last few days."

Just then a voice cried out, "Val!"

Valerie turned her head and saw another nurse beckoning her.

"Sorry, gotta go!"

Colin leaned against the wall, hands in his pockets. He let his breath out slowly and spoke softly to himself. "I'm really trying to trust You, Lord. I don't think I've ever done anything this hard before. Please give me the strength I need."

At that moment, Maggie exited one of the treatment rooms and headed for the staff lounge.

"Maggie."

She quickly turned around. Her eyes opened wide when she saw Colin.

He's here! Thank you, Lord!

"I am so glad to see you! It's been crazy here for the last few days. I haven't had a chance to call. Is everything OK?"

He smiled his familiar grin and Maggie relaxed. She was relieved to know that their previous post-dinner incident had not irreparably damaged their friendship.

"I just came to say goodbye. Is there someplace we could talk for a moment? I know you're busy, so I won't take too long." Colin's eyes reflected the sadness in his heart.

Maggie froze.

Goodbye? What does he mean by that?

"Maggie, Is there someplace private we could go?"

"Yes, yes, of course. We can go in here." Colin followed her into the staff lounge. Maggie turned around as soon as the door shut behind them.

She placed her hands on her hips and frowned. "Colin, what do you mean 'goodbye'?"

"I'm going back to England. I ... have a couple of commitments that I've been putting off for a while."

What? England? He's got to be kidding.

"You're leaving? When?" Her shoulders sagged.

Colin cleared his throat. "In a couple of hours."

Maggie's mouth dropped open.

"I tried to call you a couple of times, but you didn't answer." Colin shifted his weight from one foot to the other. "I couldn't leave without talking to you. I didn't want to leave things the way they were the other night."

"You're not leaving because of what happened, are you?"

"Well, not completely, love." He gazed at her. "I really do have a couple of contractual things I need to clear up." Colin took her hands in his and looked directly into her eyes. "I do have a request before I leave. Promise me you'll find a church ... a Bible-believing church, and you'll go ... as often as you can."

Maggie felt as though her throat was constricting.

No! He can't just walk out of my life—he can't.

She didn't know how to stop him from leaving. She had slammed that door shut four days earlier.

"I … I'll miss you," said Maggie, averting his gaze, and fighting to keep the tears from coming.

"I'll miss you, too, Maggie. I really will. One more thing. This is for you. I thought you'd like one of your own." He reached into the bag he had set on the floor and handed her a new, leather-bound Bible with her name written in gold at the bottom.

"For me?" Maggie took the Bible from his hand, then, impulsively, she hugged Colin. "Please, don't go … not like this." Unable to control herself, her tears left a trail of wet spots on his shirt.

Colin gently pulled back, then he kissed her on the forehead. "I have to, Maggie." He paused just before walking out the door. "Remember, find yourself a good church, OK?" His voice broke, and he gazed intently at her one last time before leaving.

Maggie stared at the door long after it had closed behind him. Finally, she opened her locker, glanced at the Bible in her hands, placed it inside, then slammed the door shut.

"Sis?"

Maggie froze, closing her eyes tightly, trying to control her emotions. She took a deep breath, exhaled slowly, before turning around to face her brother.

"Yes?"

"What's wrong?" asked Will, concern etched all over his rugged face. He stepped toward Maggie and pulled her over to the sofa.

"He's gone." Her voice was just above a whisper.

"Gone? Who? Colin?"

Maggie covered her mouth with her hand, focusing on nothing, and quietly spoke. "He's leaving for England today." She dropped her face into her hands. "What have I done?"

"What happened, Maggie?"

"He told me he loved me—" Her shoulders began to tremble.

"Tell me what happened."

"He told me he loved me," she repeated. "I told him I couldn't forget Scott. He said it didn't matter. But I ... I said I couldn't ... and now ... now he's gone." Maggie choked back a sob.

Just then Valerie entered the lounge.

"Hey, Will, I'll be ready in ... what's wrong?"

Will looked up. "Colin's gone."

"What do you mean 'gone'?" asked Valerie as she knelt in front of her sister-in-law. "What does he mean?"

"He went home ... to England."

Valerie glanced at her husband, who shook his head and shrugged his shoulders.

"For good?" asked Valerie. "Why? Why, Maggie?"

Maggie shook her head, her tears now flowing freely, leaving Will to answer his wife.

"Apparently, Colin told her he loved her, but ..." He turned to his sister. "Maggie, do you love Colin?" He tilted her face upward and looked into her anguished eyes.

"No, he's ... he's just a friend," she whispered, but her voice betrayed her.

"I'm not so sure he's just a friend, Sis."

Maggie shook her head fiercely. "No! I won't forget Scott!"

Will sighed. "Maggie, you don't have to forget him. Just because someone else comes into your life and you fall in love with him doesn't mean you forget those that came before. Scott will always be in your heart, forever. But there's plenty of room to love … to love *Colin*.

"What you and Scott had was amazing, but he's not here anymore, and you've got your whole life ahead of you. Scott wouldn't want you to be alone for the rest of your life, would he? If you think you love Colin, maybe you should give him a chance."

Maggie looked up at her brother and managed a weak smile. She sniffed as she spoke. "I thought you were against any kind of relationship with Colin."

"I guess I was wrong about that. He's an OK guy, and it is quite clear that he makes you very happy … well, up until now. Do you, Maggie? Do you think you love him?"

"I don't know, maybe … oh, Will, I just don't know."

"Go after him."

"What?"

"Go *after* him."

Maggie shook her head decisively. "I can't."

"Why not?" asked Valerie, taking Maggie's hands.

"I'm not off for another three hours, and by the time I'm off, he'll be gone." she whispered.

"Now, that's absurd," said Will.

"What?" Maggie looked at her brother through wet lashes.

"I said 'That's absurd.' I'm off now, and I can cover for you. The attending is still here, so I don't see a problem. I promise I'll clear it. You need to go, Maggie, and you need to go *now*."

"Mags, for once, listen to your brother." Valerie and Will stood up.

Will pulled Maggie up. "If you don't leave soon, you will miss him. Go!"

"What if he's already gone?"

"And what if he's not? Now go!"

Maggie wiped away a tear. "Why is this so hard?"

Valerie smiled, her eyes soft as she hugged her tightly and whispered in her ear, "Maybe you really do love him, Maggie."

Maggie bit her lower lip and looked at her brother. She saw the love in his eyes and hugged him. "Oh Will, what have I done?" She clung to his shirt.

"Go, Sis. You need to go." He gently pushed her away from him and toward the door.

Maggie nodded and managed a weak smile. "Thank you," she said as she turned to leave the lounge. She stopped and looked back.

"Go!" they chorused.

Maggie wiped the tears from her face. "OK, OK. I'm going!" She rushed past the nurses' station, and out through the double doors of the emergency room, wondering what she would say to Colin if she got the chance.

CHAPTER
SEVENTEEN

THE DRIVE TO the airport took longer than expected, due to the rush hour traffic and some minor road construction on Interstate 405. Maggie's heart raced as she inched her way along behind a long line of red tail lights. Finally, she began to jockey her way through the slow-moving lanes.

Forty minutes later, she parked near the private jet terminal and hurried into the airport complex. Realizing she had no ticket or boarding pass, Maggie stopped abruptly. She looked at the security checkpoint area, her heart filled with fear.

Lord, please help me. I don't know how in the world I'm going to get through security. Please, God, help me. I know You can do it, right? I mean You made the whole world in six days, so getting one person through a security check should be easy, right? Maggie swallowed hard and willed herself not to panic. *Colin always said You were with us, and You cared even about the little things. Please help me get through.*

Maybe I can say I'm his doctor. That might work. Maybe I can say he forgot some meds or something. There were four people in front of her, and no one behind her. The airport employee carefully inspected the documents of those ahead of her before motioning them forward.

Please God.

Maggie stepped up to the agent.

"Your boarding—"

"Stop him! Somebody stop him!" The piercing voice of a woman in sunglasses echoed through the security screening area.

All heads turned toward the shrill voice. Two security agents were running toward Maggie. Suddenly, directly in front of her, a small Yorki pup ran past Maggie and the security agent. Racing through the scanner, the dog's diamond studded metallic collar set off an immediate alarm. The pup circled back and ran through again.

"Don't hurt my baby!" The woman's high-pitched voice coupled with the alarms going off distracted everyone from the screening process. The agent in front of Maggie turned quickly and tried to grab the dog as it ran through the scanner a third time. He started to scurry after it, but looked up at Maggie. She was the only person left in his line.

"Come on through, quick!" said the agent as he motioned Maggie through the checkpoint. He then spun around, and sprinted after the other two security agents chasing the dog. The Yorki's owner continued to yell, and all involved were caught up in the excitement of the chase.

Maggie quickly walked through the scanner and into the terminal, afraid to look back lest the security agent call her back. Holding her breath, she marched to the private plane corridor and turned the corner, then leaned against the wall to catch her breath.

"Oh my goodness, Lord," she whispered. "I can't believe I got through. Thank You. Thank You so much."

Rushing toward the gate, she pulled out her cell phone and punched the speed dial for Colin. The call immediately went to voice mail. She tried one more time with the same results.

Text him.

She stopped and stared at her phone.

Text him.

She didn't know if she heard it or felt it, but it was undeniable and very clear. She looked at her phone once again, her hands shaking.

Pulling up her text message window, she inserted his phone number, and started moving her thumbs. After several attempts, she finally completed her message and hit the send button. She waited and watched the display.

It went blank.

Maggie shook the phone and punched the power button. Nothing happened. She repeatedly pushed the button, but her phone remained dark.

"No, no, no!" she protested loudly. "You can't be dead!" She snapped the phone shut, threw it into her purse, and rushed toward the gate.

In less than ten minutes, Maggie reached her destination. She made several inquiries and was finally told that Colin's plane had already left.

No! He can't be gone!

She stared out the window in disbelief, watching a plane ascend into the sky. Despair gripped her heart. She sank into one of the terminal chairs and continued staring out the window. Sadness overwhelmed her. She covered her face with her hands, oblivious to anyone around her, and sobbed.

"How could I have let you go?" Anguish bore down on her heart, and more tears flowed.

Exactly how long she sat in the terminal, Maggie didn't know. Finally, she sighed and wiped the tears from her face. Exhausted, she struggled to accept the fact that Colin was gone. She thought about the chaos generated by the puppy that had allowed her to walk through the security checkpoint. She stared up at the ceiling. "Why, God? Why did You let this happen?"

Lean not unto thine own understanding.

"What am I supposed to do now? Where's the 'good' in this? Colin said there's always good."

Be still, and know that I am God.

"Maybe it wasn't You at all. Maybe You only wanted Colin to experience Santa Molina and become its financial backer. Maybe You just wanted me to find You. Maybe we're not supposed to be together. Maybe—"

"Maggie?"

Maggie bolted upright. Did God just call out her name?

"Maggie?"

The voice grew louder, coming from behind her. As she turned her head, her eyes widened as her mind desperately tried to reconcile what she saw with what she had previously been told. Her mouth opened as reality pushed through her clouded mind. "Colin?"

He rushed to her. "Are you all right?" He knelt in front of her, and took her hands.

"You're here ..." She couldn't make sense of Colin's presence.

"Yes, love, I'm here. Are you OK? What's wrong?"

Maggie's voice trembled as she spoke. "I'm ... I'm fine, but your plane left. How did you ... ?"

"One of those perks I mentioned about having your own plane. I asked John to turn it around. It just took some time to get clearance to come back to the terminal, and besides ... this looked important."

He pulled his cell phone from his back pants pocket, and held it up so Maggie could see its display.

'In airport. Please don't go. Must talk.'

"How did you get that? I tried to text you, but my phone, it died."

Colin stood up and gently pulled Maggie to her feet, wrapping his arms around her. She clung to him until he loosened his hold on her and pulled back. Looking up at him through her long, black lashes, Maggie knew this was the moment that she had prayed for.

"I am so sorry, Colin. There is room in my heart for you. More than enough. Please don't go, not yet, not until we get a chance to talk." Her eyes pleaded with him.

"I'm not going anywhere, love." He cupped Maggie's face into his hands, tilted it upward, and gazed into her eyes. He hesitated for only a moment before lowering his head and kissing her tenderly. He drew her into his arms again.

"I love you, Maggie."

Joy rushed through her heart, and tears of happiness fell freely.

After another long kiss, she looked into his compassionate blue eyes, and answered, "I love you, too, Colin. I think I have for a long time … can you ever forgive me?"

Colin smiled at her and held her close. She felt his hand stroke her hair. "There is nothing to forgive, Maggie." He kissed the top of her head, and she felt his embrace tighten once more.

Although she did not know what the future held for them, Maggie truly believed, without a doubt, that God was with them, and He would direct their paths. No longer reluctant to open her heart to love, she linked her arm through his, and together, they walked out of the airport and into their future.

CPSIA information can be obtained at www.ICGtesting.com
Printed in the USA
LVOW08s0650300913

354589LV00002B/7/P